Published by Lulu for

www.connectionsbooks.co.uk

This edition first published in November 2014

Paul Stuart asserts his right to be identified as the author of this work under the Copyright, Designs and Patents Act 1988.

This novel is entirely a work of fiction.  The names, characters and incidents portrayed within it are the work of the author's imagination. Any resemblance to actual persons, living or dead, events or localities is purely coincidental. The exceptions are that The Exmoor White Horse is real, as is The Golden Horseshoe Challenge, as explained in Acknowledgements.

ISBN: 978-1-326-06979-7

## ALSO BY PAUL STUART

Connections – Who Did You Sit Next To Today? (Paperback)

Connections 2 – Hell Has No Fury. (Paperback).

The Mobile and The Ring – The John Lomax Story (Paperback)

The Mobile and The Ring – The John Lomax Story (Hardcover)

Connections 3 – That's None of Your Business (Paperback)

Lomax and The Biker – The Trilogy (Hardcover)

## ACKNOWLEDGEMENTS

This book represents another stage in the development of the Connections series, and was a different challenge for me.  It came about when my wife and I were taking a break at the Exmoor White Horse Inn, which we have been doing for some years. I was sitting at the bar early one evening before dinner, as has become my normal practice (they have, after all, over 150 whiskies and time is so short) when the owner suggested I write a novel based around the inn.  Further discussion followed, assisted by a few more drinks, and the upshot is before you. It has, of course, necessitated much research at the inn and on Exmoor.  It's been tough, but I survived!

I need to make an observation here.  The Exmoor White Horse Inn is real.  Its owners, Peter and Linda, are lovely people and have devoted over 25 years of their lives to making it a wonderful place to stay. Almost everybody who visits comes back, and many are regular returners. It must be stressed that the characters in this novel are most definitely not real and do not represent those who stay at the inn.  It would be a very strange place if they did. Of course, you never know who you are sitting next to, do you?

The Golden Horseshoe is an actual event.  Again, none of the characters in this book who enter the event or are in any way connected with it, are real, and are not meant to be representative of those who do.

My wife deserves thanks as usual for her support and, with this book, for her guidance through the perils of the whisky jungle. Yet again my family, particularly my mother and father, have been very encouraging and my friends have once again stepped up to the mark. Thank you each and every one of you.

I must also express my gratitude to Andrew and his staff at Waterstones in Truro.

Tiffany Truscott at Radio Cornwall: many thanks. There is a part waiting for you! Which one do you want?

Steve and Pete from the far north, I hope you enjoy it.

To all my friends at St Piran's in Perranarworthal...thank you from the bottom of my heart.

Finally, I should also extend my gratitude to all those who have bought my books.  I may not know all of you by name, but, please carry on!                                                           Paul

# THE SETTING

-1-

Exmoor is an area of hilly open moorland in West Somerset and North Devon, in South West England. It is named after the River Exe, which has its source in the centre of the area, two miles from Simonsbath. It is a former ancient royal hunting forest, which was given to the king in 1815.The moor has given its name to a National Park, which includes the Brendon Hills, the East Lyn Valley, The Vale of Porlock and part of the Bristol Channel coast. It is an upland of sedimentary rocks which largely date from the Devonian and early Carboniferous periods. As this area of Britain was not subject to glaciations, the plateau remains as a remarkably old landform and quartz and iron can be found in outcrops and in the subsoil. The underlying rocks are covered by moors and supported by wet, acid soil.

Exmoor has 55 kilometres (34 mi) of coastline, including the highest sea cliffs in England, which reach a height of 314 metres (1,030 ft) at Culborne Hill. However, the crest of this coastal ridge of hills is more than 1.6 km (0.99 mi) from the sea. The highest sea cliff on mainland Britain is Great Hangman near Combe Martin.

Exmoor's woodlands sometimes reach the shoreline, especially between Porlock and The Foreland, where they form the single longest stretch of coastal woodland in England and Wales.

The scenery of rocky headlands, ravines, huge waterfalls and towering cliffs gained the Exmoor coast recognition as a Heritage Coast in 1991.There are about 483 kilometres (300 mi) of named rivers on Exmoor. The River Exe rises at  Exe Head near the village of Simonsbath, close to the Bristol Channel coast, but flows more or less directly due south, so that most of its length lies in Devon. It reaches the sea at a substantial estuary on the south coast of Devon. Most other rivers arising on Exmoor flow north. The main exception to northward-draining rivers is the River Mole which arises on the south-western flanks of Exmoor. It is the major tributary of the River Taw which itself flows northward from Dartmoor. Badgworthy Water is one of the small rivers running north to the coast, and is associated with the Lorna Doone legends.

Exmoor is a magical place. The choice of activities and places of interest is endless and it offers spectacular places to walk, ride, drive or just spread out a picnic. There are also miles of coastline to explore. There is a rich variety of wildlife, including deer, otter, ravens, buzzards and the ubiquitous pheasant.

There are six species of deer established in the wild in this country. They are the red, roe, fallow, sika, muntjac and Chinese water deer. Only the red deer and roe are truly native but fallow were resident but died out and were reintroduced by either the Romans or Normans. Of the six species all except the Chinese water deer and sika have been seen within Exmoor National Park during the last ten years. Red deer are the most common on Exmoor with an annual count recording around 2,500 – 3,000 on central Exmoor. Numbers of other species can only be guessed at but roe deer are common across all Exmoor although at lower densities and may be around 1,000 in number. Fallow deer are mainly in the east of Exmoor but expanding and spreading and are likely to be under 1,000 in number. Muntjac deer numbers are small again mainly in the east but expanding and increasing. No recent validated sightings of sika deer have been reported but validated sightings of Sika have recently been made within ten kilometres of the National Park boundary.

The male red deer, Stags, are around four feet high at the shoulder and weigh about 300lbs while hinds are about three and a half feet at the shoulder and weigh around 200lbs. Only the stags have horns and these are unique to each deer. On Exmoor it is traditional to call the antlers horns even though they are not a horn but bone. The horns are cast every year and re-grow. In the wild it is unlikely many red deer live beyond 13 -14 years. The wild Exmoor red deer eat a wide variety of food including heather, whortleberry, shrubs, saplings, fruits, moss, rushes and grasses. The red deer mating season is called the rut and this is a good time to see the Exmoor red deer, especially the big old stags. After around an eight month gestation period the red deer calves are born, most in June and July with white spots for camouflage. The red deer calves can stand and feed within the hour, at four days they can outrun a man and after seven to ten days they can run with their mother. .

Red deer have lived on Exmoor for thousands of years. They used to be widespread across the whole British Isles but as the woodland which once covered our island was cut down and turned into farm land along with rapidly expanding towns and cities they lost their habitat and were extensively shot for meat and to reduce damage to crops. The end result was that the red deer disappeared from most of the British Isles except for Scotland and the south west of England. One of the main reasons the red deer survived on Exmoor was because they were protected for hunting, something which continues up to the present day. The Saxon kings hunted the wild red deer on Exmoor over 1000 years ago. When William the Conqueror took the crown he was keen on hunting and created the Royal Forest of Exmoor to protect the red deer. Exmoor was then under forest law which meant severe punishments such as blinding for those who killed Exmoor red deer without authority. Dogs kept in the boundaries of the forest had to be 'lawed', which involved cutting off three front toes so they could not be used to pursue game. Also no bows, arrows or hounds could be kept within the forest. Despite these harsh laws people still killed the Exmoor red deer and if caught would be punished by the local Swainmote court which met at Landaoro Bridge and Hawkridge churchyard or the higher court of the Forest Eyre held at Ilchester every three years. In 1508 Henry VII leased the forest to Sir Edmund Carew who had a licence to hunt the red deer. Up until the sale of the Royal forest in 1818 the forest wardens had authority to hunt the red deer, the last being Sir Thomas Ackland who was master of the North Devon staghounds. In 1811 Exmoor red deer numbers were estimated at 200 by Lord

Graves who was master of the Staghounds. In 1825 the last pack of thoroughbred Staghounds was sold to a German Baron and hunting of the Exmoor red deer stopped. In the following years without the protection of the hunts, the red deer numbers plummeted to below 100 due to poaching and shooting and the herd was in danger of extinction. In an attempt to save the Exmoor red deer, the Devon and Somerset Staghounds were formed in1855 and gradually the Exmoor red deer numbers recovered because the local people along with land owners and farmers who supported the hunt created safe areas and cover for the red deer and effectively helped to reduce shooting and poaching to save the deer for hunting. In 1881 Exmoor red deer numbers had recovered to about 500. By 1900 there were around 1,500 red deer on Exmoor but during the First World War they fell back to around 700. In 1980 Exmoor red deer numbers were estimated at 1,000, 1990 1,500 and today between 2,500 – 3,000.

Red deer have a stronghold on the moor and can be seen on quiet hillsides in remote areas, particularly in the early morning. The Emperor of Exmoor, a red stag, was Britain's largest known wild land animal, until it was killed in October 2010. The moorland habitat is also home to hundreds of species of birds, including

Merlin, Peregrine Falcon, Raven Buzzard, Curlew, Stonechat and many more.

There is a legend that tells of the existence of the Beast of Exmoor and there have been numerous reports of eyewitness sightings. However the BBC calls it "the famous-yet-elusive beast of Exmoor." Sightings were first reported in the 1970s, although it became notorious in 1983, when a South Molton farmer claimed to have lost over 100 sheep in the space of three months, all of them apparently killed by violent throat injuries. Descriptions of its colouration range from black to tan or dark grey. It is possibly a cougar or black leopard, which was released after a law was passed in 1976 making it illegal for them to be kept in captivity outside zoos. In 2006, the British Big Cats Society reported that a skull found by a Devon farmer was that of a Puma.

## THE EXMOOR WHITE HORSE INN

-2-

My wife and I take a short break here about twice each year. We discovered this oasis of calm purely by chance on the way back from a journey further north.  I was too tired to complete the drive and we dropped into a Tourist Information Centre, searching for a place to stay for one night.  We were directed to The Exmoor White Horse Inn at Exford. I am certain it was meant to be. We have found a place that we would rather keep for ourselves, but it seems far too many people are already party to the secret.

Located in the village of Exford, not far as the crow flies from Dunkery Beacon, The Exmoor White Horse Inn may be found. This jewel is 26 miles from junction 25 of the M5 motorway. It can be found by following the A358 from Taunton towards Minehead for about 3 miles and then turning left along the B3224. After about 10 miles, at Raleighs Cross (pub) the route takes a right turn, following the B3224 which changes course here. After about 6 miles Wheddon Cross appears and the signs to Exford are picked up.  They take the traveller straight across the crossroads and onward for the final 5 miles to Exford.

The inn nestles by the bridge on the River Exe, and is a traditional 16th century building, festooned in Virginia Creeper. Inside there are log fires and a fine restaurant which uses locally sourced produce.  The Head Chef produces a menu replete with meats from rare breed cattle, west-country seafood and moorland game. Another compelling feature is the bar, which boasts over 150 malt whiskies. So much to do; so little time!   There are 28 bedrooms, each with its own plethora of stories and anecdotes. Have you ever wondered who has stayed in your hotel room whenever you check in?  Which room did you stay in? If only it could speak!

In the same way that rooms have histories, so the people who stay in them also carry personal baggage as well as their luggage. Have you ever thought that you booome part of that history from the moment you make the booking? Each and every visitor has tales to be told, but most prefer to keep them to themselves. What about you?

# HAYLEY THE RECEPTIONIST

-3-

Hayley, Receptionist at The Exmoor White Horse Inn, was well liked both by customers and staff. She was petite, pretty and had a certain way about her; perfect credentials for the job. She had been there for a few years and was efficient and friendly. Although not originally from the area, she had grown to love and become part of it.  Her boyfriend, a local man, doted upon her and would move heaven and earth to grant her every wish. They had been together for about two years and had reached the stage of their relationship when decisions would soon need to be made. Marriage? Babies? See the world? Start a business of their own? Carry on, happy as they undoubtedly were?

Hayley's main love, apart from her boyfriend, was her horse. She had inherited him from her sister when she decided to go travelling abroad. His name was Hal, or to give him his full title, Prince Halberad theThird of somewhere or other. He was a thoroughbred Arab stallion, had a glossy pitch black coat and stood proud and tall, as if he knew of his lineage. His manner was haughty and he could also be temperamental. Hayley wished she could have ridden him in The Golden Horseshoe, but he wasn't an endurance horse. He was, to put it simply, just a magnificent specimen.

Her boyfriend did not share her love of the magnificent animal. He resented the time required to look after him and the love she invested in him. In short, he was jealous.  He knew it was stupid to be jealous of a horse, but he couldn't help it. He was a rival; there was no other way to dress it up. He was also afraid of the beast. In his mind it was decision time about the horse as well as anything else.

They say that you should be careful what you wish for. Hayley tested that maxim one evening as she indulged her other love: fast cars. She had treated herself to a hot car, and loved giving it the beans and testing her driving skills. She still had the metal pins in her right arm as evidence of the passion. The accident happened on the A396 near Bampton at the Black Cat junction. They were returning to Exford at the end of a good night out and Hayley was showing off her skills to her new boyfriend. The road was wet and muddy. Landslips were common there and works were in progress to construct a wall, with rod insertions, at the junction. Three-way traffic lights were in place to control the flow of vehicles bound for Bampton and Dulverton. The lights, however, failed that night and

Hayley ploughed her speeding pride and joy straight into the partly constructed wall, in order to avoid an oncoming heavy lorry. The thought flashed through her mind that it was the lesser of two evils. She was probably correct, even though she broke her arm in two places and suffered some nasty cuts and bruises. Her boyfriend was luckier and escaped with a cut to his left leg, badly torn jeans and heavy bruising to his gentleman's private area. She needed surgery, whilst he needed tender loving care and plenty of ice. Thankfully, she had not been drinking that night, even though the police suspected she had. They argued that there was no reason for her to have gone through a red light unless she had been influenced by drink or was otherwise distracted. It didn't take long to prove the lights were faulty, but the argument about admission of guilt by the contractor or local authority was an entirely different matter. In fact, it still hasn't been resolved after two years.

Hayley had omitted to include something in her account of the accident, because she couldn't believe it herself. In the instant before her car had hit the wall she thought she saw a man dressed as a highwayman. By the time she gathered her senses after the smash, she doubted whether she had seen anything at all. She had also omitted something else. She knew she had not swerved to avoid an oncoming heavy lorry. She knew she had swerved to avoid what she now knew was a stagecoach. She had only ever told her boyfriend about these two mysterious facts, and was upset when he dismissed them out of hand.

As proof of her popularity her boss at The White Horse, Linda, was constantly offering to let her drive her own car. The Scooby was, as far as Hayley was concerned, lightning fast. It was recognised throughout the locality, and Linda's speed was also well known and feared by all around. Indeed, when Linda declared her intention to take a drive somewhere, most sensible people studiously avoided being anywhere near. This made the roads even clearer for her, apart from unwitting visitors, many of whom had a close shave as they felt the rush of her passing. Linda was becoming a legend on Exmoor. Hayley would have loved to give it a go, but didn't trust herself with it and now contented herself with adrenalin fuelled rides in the passenger seat from time to time.

Hayley was a model employee. She was always punctual and stayed late when needed, often without being asked. She was pretty, neat and trim. She had been a hit with the customers from the day she walked into The Exmoor White Horse. In short, she was perfect.

Hayley's boyfriend also understood that the time was coming when they would need to make choices. They had been together for two years and he thought he loved her, but wasn't sure what love actually is.  He couldn't define it; he only recognised when it was not there. He knew he had never been so content and in an ideal world, his world, things would stay just as they were. The trouble was that she seemed to be itching for something more. He didn't mind her love of fast cars, despite the fact that it had almost killed the pair of them. He knew she was happy in her job.  The more he thought about it, the more he realised that the problem was her damn horse. He believed she loved it more than she loved him. It took up a disproportionate amount of her time.

Her daily routine was to get out of bed at five in the morning and make a cup of tea for herself. She tried not to disturb him, so he didn't warrant a cup of tea in bed. She then took herself off to the stables, where she spent at least two hours doing whatever was needed to make sure the beast was fed, watered and groomed.

She may have done other things there, but it was all a mystery to

him. He once threatened to accompany her to help, to take an

interest, but she flatly refused his offer, saying it was her horse,

her responsibility and anyway she knew he hated Hal. It caused

tension in the house for over a week, so he withdrew the offer and

the climate warmed again. Her routine continued with a rushed

breakfast, again without a thought for him, and a rapid exit and

fast drive to work. At the end of her shift she went straight to the

stables and exercised her beloved Hal for at least an hour before

bedding him down for the night. By the time she arrived home, she

was already dead beat and usually prepared a hurried meal for the

two of them, before collapsing into a chair in front of the TV and

promptly falling asleep.  He usually had to rouse her to make sure

she went to bed rather than sleeping there all night. He had

offered to make the evening meal, to take the pressure off

somewhat, but he was a useless cook and it didn't work. Now

whenever she complained of being exhausted, he told her in no uncertain terms that it was her fault because she chose to lead her life like that. He had no sympathy; she could change things but chose not to.

It was the little things. He assumed it was the same in most relationships; always the little things that were the clues. He knew Hayley was a fast driver and could get home from the stables in about 20 minutes, but now took about an hour. What did she do in the other 40 minutes? Where did she go? Then there were the phone calls. He'd sometimes come home and find her on the phone. Admittedly she'd smile and blow him a kiss, but it seemed that the tone of her voice would change as soon as she saw him and she'd hang up soon after. So he would take a shower and pretend to forget a clean towel and call for her to get one for him, and when she disappeared into the laundry room he'd go into the kitchen and debate for a few seconds but then he'd go ahead and hit redial on the phone. Sometimes it turned out to be a neighbour or her mother; sometimes nobody picked up. He remembered seeing a film about spies or something, in which one person would call somebody else and they'd let it ring twice then call back exactly one minute later and he knew it was safe to pick up. Hayley's boyfriend tried to work out the numbers she was calling from the sound of the dialling but they went too fast. He'd be embarrassed because he was acting so paranoid, but then there'd be another little thing and he'd get suspicious again. Lately he thought she'd been coming home with the smell of wine on her breath and he tried to snatch an unexpected kiss just to make sure, but she would pull away.  It was as if the spontaneity, the passion, had gone. He tried to put a finger on it but couldn't explain it.

His suspicions smacked of midlife crisis, but he knew they were too young for that. Sometimes in life you have to be smart. He hadn't really found any proof. He really thought her commitment to the horse was wearing her out and there was no more to it than that. And yet the doubts would not disappear. If she was straying he wondered where she found the time or energy. Her life revolved around her work and her horse, and it seemed to him that he was no longer an important part in it. He'd always thought of her as absolutely loyal; sin free, but the thought nagged at him that even saints sin sometimes.

He maintained his checks on her, looking for the little things until one day he found a big thing.

It was five-thirty and Hayley had phoned to say she was going to be late because she was going shopping after dealing with the horse. He told her not to rush, to take all the time she wanted. He didn't tell her he was going to go through their bedroom, searching for something that had been bothering him all day. That morning he had walked quietly past the bedroom where she was getting dressed and peered in. He saw her take an object out of her bag and hide it in the bottom drawer of her dresser. After half an hour of ransacking and prowling through every conceivable hiding place in the room he found what he was looking for. It was a sealed red card envelope, but there was no name or address on the front. He didn't know what to make of it and the more he held it, the heavier it seemed to become, almost like a physical burden. He turned it over and over in his hands and studied it carefully.  She hadn't licked the flap completely so he could pry most of it open but he couldn't get at it fully without tearing the paper. He found an old razor blade and spent an age carefully scraping away at the glue on the flap.

At six-thirty, with the last little bit to go, the phone rang. It was Hayley and, for once, he was relieved to hear her say that she was going to be even later than she thought because she'd met an old school friend and was going to stop for a drink with her on the way home. She asked if he wanted to join them, but he said he was too tired. He hurried back to finish his project. Finally, he scraped off the last of the glue and with shaking hands opened the flap. He pulled the card out. On the front was a picture of a Victorian couple, holding hands and looking out over a snowy backyard as candles glowed around them. He took a deep breath and opened the card. It was blank. He knew at that moment that all his fears were true. There was only one reason to give somebody a blank card and that was the fear of being caught.

It wasn't the little things any more. He knew without doubt that she was seeing someone and probably had been for months. He tore the card into little pieces, flung them across the room and fell back on the bed. He stared at the ceiling for a full half an hour trying to calm himself, but the rage would not abate. He knew where she was likely to be for her drink with 'an old school friend' so he set out to find them. It didn't take long. He found them at the first attempt. She was sitting there with her lover and he tasted the familiar metallic flavour of his anger. He wanted to scream.

He spun away from the window and strode through the front door. There was a man sitting with her at a table.

Hayley saw him and with a sharp intake of breath, gasped, "what are you doing here?"

He muttered, "When you cheat on somebody there are consequences."

"What do you mean, cheat?" she said, aghast at the suggestion.

There was movement to his left and he spun to meet it. He recognised Hayley's old school friend immediately as she sat beside the man and kissed him on the cheek. Both wore wedding rings.

"You didn't think...?" said Hayley.

Her boyfriend said nothing. He was too embarrassed to speak.

"You idiot!" Hayley said. "I was out tonight buying you a birthday present. I've been rotten to you lately and I wanted to show you I still love you." She pointed to a shopping bag at her feet.

"Did you buy me a card as well?" he asked.

"Of course," Hayley was fighting back tears.

"Is that the one in your drawer at home?"

She blinked. "Yes, it's for you."

"Then why is it sealed and blank?"

Her tears stopped and her face blossomed with anger. "I didn't seal it. The flap got wet in the bathroom and I put it away to sort out later. I didn't want you to find it."

It was as if somebody had flicked a switch. He towered over the table and landed and huge blow on the man sitting there. Twenty minutes later, and after much cursing and a sprawling fight, he was arrested by two burly policemen who had reacted swiftly to the emergency call. There was a good deal of blood on the floor.

He was charged and found guilty of GBH, Assault and several other lesser offences. Hayley gave evidence and her account of life with him made harrowing listening. His long history of depression, paranoid behaviour and uncontrolled temper came to light. The court sent him to a secure hospital to serve his sentence.

She only sent him one letter. To be more accurate, it was a card. The only words it contained were "It's not just the little things."

Ironically her boyfriend had been correct. She had been seeing somebody else. His name was Philippe and he worked at the White Horse with her.

## AN UNUSUAL BOOKING

### -4-

"I'd like to go to Exmoor for a few days."

"You mean," she looked over at him, slightly disturbed by his sudden announcement, "to see Philippe?"

Cheryl Andrews looked carefully at her fingernails, which she was painting bright red. This ritual happened too often as far as he was concerned. He wondered for what, or for whom, she prepared herself so fastidiously. He had come to loathe the colour, but had never told her so.

"That's not a bad idea," she said eventually. "You'd enjoy yourself. Perhaps he'll take you up on the Moor and you can shoot some pheasant. "

"I don't think he'd do that," he said. "He prefers to walk and finds out of the way places. He's not into shooting, and anyway I'm not sure it's legal, or even if it's the right season."

"Where will you stay? He's hardly got enough room to swing a cat." Cheryl tried to take the words back, but it was too late.

"I'll see if he can get me a room at The White Horse.  You know; that lovely place in Exford we went to once. I've always wanted to go back there. He works there, so if there's a spare room going,

I'm sure he'll get me in." Graeme Andrews said, choosing to make no comment on her slip, preferring to file it for future reference. He sat across from her on the wooden decking at the rear of their house on the outskirts of Hereford, looking out towards the Malvern Hills in the distance. He was struck by the thought that she had not questioned the fact that he wanted to go on his own. The month was June and the air was thick with the smell of gorse. Graeme used to like that smell. Now, however, it made him sick to his stomach.

Cheryl inspected her nails for streaks and pretended to be comfortable with the idea of him going to see Philippe. He'd often invited them back to Exford since their first visit, but they had never managed to make it happen and now he had suddenly suggested he would like to go alone. The telltale signs of tension began to flutter in her stomach. He looked at her, searching for clues. She was not a good actress. He could tell she was excited at the thought of a few days to herself and he thought he knew the reason. He did not let her know. He just watched the midges and kept quiet. Unlike her, he could act. He had learned that skill from an early age.

They were silent and sipped their drinks, ice cubes clinking sharply in their crystal glasses. It was the first day of summer and there must've been a thousand insects around.

"I know I promised to clean up the garage," he said, working on his acting skills, "but I'll do it when I get back."

"That's OK; I think it's a great idea, going back there." Cheryl said, too enthusiastically for his liking. "I'll spend the time painting my dressing room. I'd rather do that myself anyway."

I knew you'd think it'd be a good idea, Graeme thought, but said nothing to her. Lately he'd been thinking a lot of things and not saying them. He was sweating, but it was more from excitement than from the heat and he wiped the moisture from his face and his shortcut blond hair with a napkin.

The phone rang and Cheryl went to answer it. She came back and said, "It's your father" in that sour voice of hers. She sat down and didn't say anything else; just picked up her drink and examined her nails again.

Graeme got up and went into the kitchen. His father lived in Durham, hundreds of miles away. He loved the man and wished they lived closer together. Cheryl, however, didn't like him one bit and always made a fuss when Graeme wanted to visit. Graeme was never exactly sure what the problem was between Cheryl and his father, but it annoyed him greatly that she seemed to treat him badly and would never talk to Graeme about it. It sometimes got to the point that he even felt guilty he had a father. He enjoyed talking but hung up after only five minutes because he felt she didn't want him to be on the phone. He then made a call of his own.

He walked out onto the decking. "I've just spoken to Philippe. There's a spare room from Saturday. I could go then."

Cheryl said, "I think Saturday would be fine."

They went inside and watched TV for a while. Then, at eleven Cheryl looked at her watch, stretched and said, "It's getting late. Time for bed." When she said that there was no room for argument.

Later that night, when Cheryl was asleep, he walked downstairs into the study. He reached behind a row of books resting on the built-in bookshelves and pulled out a large, sealed envelope. He carried it out to his workshop. He had found it in the true crime section of a local book shop. He had never stolen anything in his life but that day he'd looked around the store and slipped the book inside his jacket and strolled casually out of the shop. He'd had to steal it as he was afraid that somebody might remember him buying the book and that could be used against him later.

Graeme knew nothing about crime apart from what he'd seen on TV or read in books. He believed none of the criminals seemed very clever and they were usually caught, even though they seemed only marginally less smart that their pursuers. It seemed to him that they always left too many clues. The book he was reading, however, was different. It was extremely detailed and gave a good deal of information about police procedure and thinking.  Surely it contained what he was looking for. He knew he needed to deal with Philippe and he had to find a foolproof method. He had been thinking about the problem ever since he and Cheryl had spent time at The White Horse and she and Philippe had become "good friends."  It had been eating away at him ever since and his unease increased as she mentioned him at every opportunity. Graeme noticed that Cheryl was starting to spend a good deal of time on the phone and online. He tried to check the phone bills to find out whether she was calling him, but she threw them away.  He tried to read her e-mails as well, but she changed the password. He was, however, computer literate, and easily hacked into her account. Again, she was one step ahead because she deleted them all on the main server. It so infuriated him that he almost smashed the computer into pieces.

He walked back upstairs, packed the book in the bottom of his suitcase and lay on the couch in the study, looking out of the window at the hazy summer stars and thinking about his trip to Exmoor from every angle.

Everything was changing. Cheryl and Graeme still had dinner together but it wasn't the same as it used to be. They didn't have picnics, they had stopped taking walks in the evenings and they hardly ever sat together on the decking anymore. He told Cheryl that he didn't like Philippe, but she told him to stop being jealous as there was nothing for him to worry about. Graeme, though, could not help himself and continued to worry.  The feeling became worse when he found a post it note in her purse last month. It said CC-Monday 2pm.

"I'm going shopping tomorrow," Cheryl had told him. "I fancy some retail therapy."

"Where?" he asked, his suspicion alerted.

"Cribbs Causeway, I think," she replied, "so I'll be gone all day."

He didn't want to make her suspicious, so he said cheerfully, "ok. Good idea. You'll enjoy that. I'll look after myself here."

As soon as her car had pulled out of the drive the next morning, he began calling motels in the area around the Cribbs Causeway shopping complex, asking to speak to Philippe Delon. The fourth came up trumps.

"One moment please, I'll put you through."

Graeme hung up quickly. He couldn't drive, so he phoned for a taxi from the local company with which Cheryl maintained an account.  He was not far behind her when he parked in the motel's car park. He saw her car there, parked without a care in the world just in front of the entrance.  It seemed to mock him and he gripped the seat as he fought his rising anger. He walked to Reception and was told the room number he sought after saying he had a gift for the couple, and wanted to surprise them.

He crept close to the partly open window. The curtains were drawn and his anger almost boiled over. He had a struggle to bear down on it. He could hear parts of the conversation.

"I don't like that colour. I want you to paint your nails red. It's sexy. I don't like that colour you're wearing. What is it?"

"Peach."

"I like bright red," Philippe said.

"Well, ok."

There was some laughing, followed by a long silence.

Graeme tried to look inside but couldn't see anything.

Finally, Cheryl said, "we have to talk about Graeme. He knows something. I know he does. He's been like a spy lately. Sometimes I'd like to strangle him."

Outside the window Graeme closed his eyes. He pressed the lids closed so hard that he thought he might never open them again. He heard the sound of a can opening.

Philippe said, "so what does it matter if he does find out?"

"I've been thinking about it. I think you should do something with him."

"Do something with him?" Philippe had an edge to his voice, "what do you mean?"

"Invite him to Exmoor. You know how he likes to walk and you could show him some interesting places, I'm sure. Get to know him. Prove to him that we're just good friends and there's nothing for him to worry about. That way, we'll be in the clear to carry on." Cheryl was at her convincing best.

"You are joking!" he replied.

"No, ask us both to come. I'll find a reason not to be able to make it. He'll have to come by himself."

"That means I have to pretend I like him."

"Yes, that's exactly what it means. It's not going to kill you."

"Pick another weekend. You come with him."

"No," she said. "I'd have trouble keeping my hands off you."

There was a long pause, punctuated by much rustling and sighing, before Graeme heard Philippe say, "Oh, all right, I'll do it."

It took all Graeme's willpower not to scream.

He hurried home, threw himself down on the couch in the study and turned on the TV. When Cheryl came home he pretended he'd fallen asleep. Cheryl's shopping episode was the precursor to Graeme's acceptance of Philippe's invitation to spend a few days at The White Horse.

"Drive carefully," said Cheryl as he climbed into the car.

"Don't worry I will," replied the taxi driver, barely able to complete his words before Graeme urged him to accelerate away.

It was not a long drive from Hereford to Exford and Graeme actually enjoyed the scenery and being able to listen to his own choice of music. The Doors blasted out from the sound system and he sang and tapped his fingers.

He turned it down as the car pulled into the car park of The White Horse. After booking in, he unpacked in his room and strolled down to the bar to meet Philippe, as arranged.

"Welcome," said Philippe in that French accent that most women, and certainly Cheryl, find sexy. "It's good to see you again."

"It's good to see you too," lied Graeme as he shook the outstretched hand.

"I thought we'd eat here tonight," said Philippe. "I've booked a table, but there's time for a drink or two."

"Sounds good to me," replied Graeme. "But it's soft drinks only for me, if I'm to be any use tomorrow," he joked.

"Which room are you in?" asked his host and Philippe told him.

They stayed in the bar and chatted for an hour, killing time before their evening meal. Graeme felt uncomfortable spending time with him, whilst Philippe felt equally ill at ease because he realised that Graeme must know their secret and still accepted his invitation. They made their plans for a walk on the Moor for the next day.  Philippe was due to be working the early shift, including breakfast, and would be free from about 11am, so they planned to take a packed lunch and spend the rest of the day hiking.

"Good morning," Philippe called, as Graeme sat watching the fish lazily swimming to and fro in the River Exe as it wandered past the front of the hotel and out of site under the bridge.

"Hello," replied Graeme.

"I hope your room was to your liking, and the breakfast up its usual standard," Philippe enquired.

"The room is perfect. I like the outlook over the front, with the river. There's a sense of calm. The breakfast was excellent; just as I remember it," answered Graeme. "I don't think I'll need to eat anything else for the rest of the day."

"Well, chef's done us proud for lunch as well," said Philippe, indicating a backpack that looked full to bursting.

"So, where are we going?" Graeme asked.

"I thought we'd take it gently to start with, seeing as it's your first day and you're not used to long walks," said Philippe, mocking his guest.

Graeme did not take well to the mockery, which he thought was meant to be patronising. "Don't you worry about me, I'll keep up wherever you take me," he said with a determined note of defiance.

"Well if you're sure," Philippe said. "I thought we'd take a look at Tar Steps for lunch and then go on to Hawkridge and back here. Exford is fairly central, so it works quite well. It'll be a long walk, but the scenery is fantastic and the weather looks good."

They set off at a brisk pace with the Frenchman into his best walking guide mode, clearly enjoying himself.  Suddenly he stopped. "Nobody knows about this place. I found it by myself," he announced proudly, sounding like he had found a cure for cancer. "Let's see if I can still do it."  He produced a pistol before Graeme could react and fired a round. Crack. Just like that, with not a care that it might be heard. He frowned because he had missed his target. "I'm rusty, I haven't done this for a long time," he said, grinning at Graeme.

He dug into his backpack and pulled out a second pistol, which he handed to Graeme. "You have a go. See if you can hit that can over there."

Graeme was lost for words, but accepted the challenge. Crack. He missed as well. Graeme fired again and hit the can, which leapt into the air. He couldn't stop a cry of excitement.

They reloaded and walked on. Philippe challenged him to hit a rock some thirty feet away, but Graeme missed with every shot.

"Not bad," Philippe said. "You were close with the last couple." Graeme knew he was being sarcastic.

They reloaded again and walked on again.

"So," Philippe asked, "how's she doing?"

"Fine. She's fine." He meant that he didn't feel like discussing her or telling him anything. His hands were sweaty and he ground his teeth together.

"Did she get her car fixed?" Philippe asked, "she was saying that there was something wrong with the brakes."

Graeme was shocked. Her car had only broken down a few days ago, so how did he know? He made no reply, but Philippe repeated the question.

"Oh, her car? Yeah, it's okay. She took it in and they fixed it."

He looked at Philippe's tanned face and tried to work him out. He looked sort of innocent, but Graeme had learned that people who seemed innocent were sometimes the most guilty. He scoured his surroundings.

"What are you looking for?" asked Philippe.

"Something to shoot," replied Graeme. He wasn't. He was making sure there would be no witnesses. "Let's go that way," he suggested as he walked towards a fence.

"OK, that's the right way anyway," said Philippe.

Graeme studied it as they approached and was pleased to spot the wooden posts about five feet apart and the strands of rusting wire. It would be not too easy to climb over, but it wasn't barbed wire like some of the fences they had already passed. Graeme didn't want it to be too easy to climb. He'd been thinking. He had a plan. He had been thinking about it for quite a while and had it indelibly fixed in his brain. "So what does she do?" he asked.

What does who do?" replied Philippe.

"Your girlfriend," said Graeme.

Philippe was momentarily put off guard by the sudden change of direction in the conversation. "Um, oh, she works in Bristol."

"Oh," said Graeme, and left it at that.

They were closer to the fence and he was looking around again. Not for rabbits, or any targets, but for witnesses. The fence was now only twenty feet away.

"Look, over there," Graeme pointed over the other side of the fence.

"What?" asked Philippe.

"Rabbits. Come on, I'll show you."

They walked the rest of the way to the fence. Suddenly Philippe reached out and took Graeme's pistol. "I'll hold it while you climb over. It's safer that way."

Graeme froze with terror. He realised that Philippe was about to do exactly what he himself had planned. He was going to hold Philippe's pistol and shoot him when he was at the top of the fence. It would look like a tragic accident; that he had tried to carry it as he climbed the fence but he'd dropped it and it had gone off. He was betting on the old adage that what looks like an accident probably is an accident. Graeme didn't move. He thought he saw something odd in Philippe's eyes, something mean and terrible. He looked at the eyes and understood at that moment how much Philippe hated him. He also realised just how much he loved Cheryl. Moments of great fear often crystallise things; they certainly strip them down to the bare essentials. People should remember those moments because they can inform future actions.

"You want me to go first?" Graeme asked. He wondered if he should simply run.

"Yes," said Philippe. "You go first, and then I'll hand the backpack and guns over to you." What he said and the message Graeme received were very different.  He was really asking

Graeme whether he was afraid of climbing over the fence with his back to him. Perhaps he should just run.

Then Philippe was looking around too. Searching for witnesses, just as Graeme had been.

"Go on," Philippe encouraged.

Graeme, his hands shaking with fear, began to climb. He knew he was about to be shot, but could do nothing to prevent it. He put his foot on the first rung of wire and started to ascend. His heart was beating a million times a minute and he had to pause to wipe his hands. He thought he heard a whisper, as if Philippe was talking to himself. He swung his leg over the top strand of wire. He thought he heard the sound of a pistol being readied.

"You're dead!" Philippe said, in a hoarse whisper. You're dead.'

Graeme gasped.

Crack!

The short snappy sound filled the air. Graeme choked back a cry and looked around, nearly falling from his precarious perch astride the top wire.

"Merde!" Philippe muttered. He was aiming away from the fence and nodded towards a tree line. "Rabbit. Missed him by two inches."

His hands still shaking, Graeme continued over the fence and climbed to the ground on the other side.

"Are you ok?" Philippe asked, "you look a little funny."

"I'm fine," he said. "fine, fine."

Philippe handed over the backpack and two guns. He began to climb. Graeme debated and gripped Philippe's gun tightly. He walked over to the fence so that he was immediately underneath his foe.

"Look!" Philippe said. He was straddled over the top if the fence. "Over there." He pointed nearby. A large rabbit was standing on its haunches less than twenty feet away. "Come on, you've got a great shot. "

Graeme raised the gun.

"Go on, what are you waiting for?" demanded Philippe from on high.

He was moments away from committing the perfect murder. Graeme looked at Philippe and then the rabbit.

"Are you going to shoot?" asked Philippe.

He raised the gun and pulled the trigger once.  Philippe gasped and pressed at the tiny bullet hole in his chest. He fell backwards off the fence and lay on a patch of dried mud, completely still. The rabbit, panicked by the noise, bounded away across the Moor.

On his way home, Graeme took special care to dispose of the book. It had served its purpose. He saw Cheryl as he arrived in the taxi. She looked numb. She wore dark glasses and looked like she had been crying. She was clutching a sodden tissue in her fingers. Her nails were not bright red anymore and they weren't peach either. They were just plain fingernail colour. Graeme was reminded of the time when his parents were divorced. She had looked exactly the same. He steeled himself to be an actor once more.

"I've got bad news," she said as he climbed from the car. "Philippe's been badly hurt in a hunting accident."

He looked at her and decided it would be better to say nothing.

"Apparently, he fell from the top of a fence and his gun went off," she said.

That's pretty accurate Graeme thought. "Was he your boyfriend?" he asked.

"No, of course he wasn't," she replied, a little too quickly. "He was just a good friend."

Graeme pulled a face at her.

"What's the matter? Aren't I allowed to have any friends?"

Graeme thought for a moment and was sorely tempted to reply. No, you are not; most certainly not. You're not going to get away with dumping your son the way you dumped Dad.

"Why don't we have a holiday, just the two of us,?" Graeme suggested, his mind already moving on.

"Where?" Cheryl asked.

"Oh, I thought a few days at The Exmoor White Horse might be fun," Graeme suggested and smiled as he turned away.

## THE GOLDEN HORSESHOE

-5-

In such a setting horse riding has become a way of life, so it is fitting that it is now the location for the most challenging endurance riding event in Great Britain.

The 50th anniversary of the Golden Horseshoe ride and of endurance riding in Great Britain was a special event.  It was highlighted in the diaries and on the calendars of many equine enthusiasts from Lands End to John O'Groats, and beyond. There were special classes to celebrate the landmark event, and some of the original riders from the first event returned to enhance the occasion.

Although there are records of a few organised 'Long Distance Rides' before the second World War, one of which was organised by Country Life and Riding Magazine in 1938, the sport of endurance riding appears to have kept a low profile until 1965. During that summer The British Horse Society ran its first Golden Horseshoe Ride on Exmoor, promoted by author Ronald Duncan and Col. Mike Ansell, and sponsored by the Sunday Telegraph.

The idea was so popular that organisers had to close entries a month early, having reached the limit of 110 entrants.

The route was linear, starting at Malmsmead, and finishing at Mr Duncan's home in Welcombe, Devon. There were no markers, and riders had to find their own way, including navigating across 'The Chains' with the help of several local people riding Exmoor ponies. There was also no minimum speed and one couple were seen to have their own chauffeured car following them on the roads, enabling them to stop for a picnic on the way. At the finish, Glenda Spooner and John Oaksey were waiting to check the horses to ensure that they were in good condition and all who completed at 6mph or above received a gold-painted horseshoe. The Golden Horseshoe Ride was born, and organisers and participants agreed that it was a really good test of a horse's fitness, and rider's horsemanship.

Originally, the event moved to a different location each year, including Brighton and Yorkshire, until 1974 when it returned to Exmoor permanently, and became based in Oxford.

The ride became more 'organised' in succeeding years, with routes being marked first of all with  painted horseshoes fixed on poles, and later by Jim Collins of the Exmoor National Park

Authority with flags made out of fertiliser bags, which 'marched across the moor' to give excellent visibility, except for when the Exmoor mist descended!

As is often the way with developing sports, the rules became increasingly stringent, with speeds of 8mph or above required to achieve a Gold award. Vetting procedures also improved to ensure that the horses were protected from abuse.

The modern event has seven competitive classes from which to choose, and the ride is a far cry from that first fifty mile competition. Routes are carefully planned and clearly marked; nobody stops to indulge in picnics along the way; vets are in attendance before and after each day's rides; communications are modern; St John's Ambulance is on standby and each horse and rider has their own support dashing across the moor, mostly in 4x4's, to be ready with water and food whenever needed. Local people buzz around on Quad bikes like demented hornets. Spectators speed along the narrow lanes of the moor, using the support teams as guides in an effort to reach vantage points from which to view. Some are caught up in the event for the first time simply because it coincided with their break on Exmoor and their very unsuitable vehicles take a particular pounding. Other better prepared more regular and devoted followers, lead the chase to each checkpoint, with seasoned nonchalance.

Riders prepare carefully as it has become the most challenging event of its type in the country.  Horse and rider are qualified to compete in whichever class they have entered, before the first step of the event is even taken, so basic fitness is not, in theory, an issue. However, Exmoor, whilst stunningly beautiful, can also be dangerous. It is a unique National Park, with breathtaking moorland that runs from the spectacular cliffs at the edge of the Atlantic Ocean to the historic pastures rolling inland.

It has a greater variety of terrain than almost any other ride the competitors will have previously encountered and serious hill training is part of anybody's wise preparations. Horses also need to be comfortable going through water, which can be chest deep at times. Horse and rider need also to be sure they can both go out for two days consecutive hard riding.

The weather inevitably plays a major part in the event.  Exmoor weather is notoriously fickle and virtually all kinds of conditions may be encountered, so both horse and rider need to be catered for. Tack and clothing for the horse needs to include a breast plate as a sweaty horse going up a steep hill is an invitation for the saddle to slip, spare reins because if very wet, the original ones may need to be swapped, several numnahs, at least two of every imaginable kind of rug, electrolytes and as many water carriers as can be managed. Stable bandages for the evenings and in between and after the end of the competition are also recommended by the organisers.

Riders often need to change clothing halfway round the course, so the support team needs to be prepared.  Finally, sun block may even be needed if Exmoor decides to be kind.

## THE BUILD UP

-6-

Most competitors like to learn about the history of the event before taking part, as well as gathering information and seeking as much advice as possible. Lisa Richards and Karen Wilson, along with their support teams were no different. For all of them it meant taking several rooms at The Exmoor White Horse Inn, in each case for a week's stay. Lisa Richards chose a large room for herself, booked a further three rooms for her support team, which numbered six in total and paid for them all. It was, after all, the beginning of a new life for her.  Karen and Kevin Wilson returned to the room in the Lodge with the babbling River Exe at the bottom of the garden.  It brought back wonderful, poignant memories of their last hurrah the previous November. The cost was of no consequence to them because they had long since learned that there are more important things in life than money.  Kevin had come to the conclusion that the only people in the world who didn't care about what things cost were those for whom it made no difference. Sadly, that now included him and Karen, albeit for a terrible reason.

Also sitting down to dinner in the restaurant was a party of tourists on a package tour from America. None of them had met before their trip as it was specifically aimed at single people of a "certain age" for whom money was no object. They were eight in number and their table was set diagonally across one of the two restaurant dining rooms, so that other tables, set for two, four or more people, were fitted around the edges of the room. At one of these tables sat a couple who were regular visitors.  They stayed at The Exmoor White Horse Inn twice each year and usually occupied the Honeymoon Suite, even though they were in their late fifties or early sixties.  Two men from Manchester were due to sit at another table for two. They were only partners in the business sense and were not on a break, though they wished they were.  Dennis and Vince were there because a local church had contracted them to install electric under-pew heating.  The work was scheduled to take about five days, so they had arrived on the Sunday afternoon, ready to begin the next day. Dennis was also scouting for a location for his forthcoming wedding and he wanted to surprise his bride to be.

In fact every room at the inn was fully occupied for the entire week, so the restaurant, bar and lounge were a hive of activity.

Locals also added to the atmosphere, mostly sitting on stools at the bar and chatting to each other, the barman and, occasionally, a visitor or two. One such visitor would be Quentin Legard. Remember that name.

## LISA RICHARDS

### -7-

Lisa Richards was killing two birds with one stone as she turned her car onto the road which would eventually take her on the first part of her journey from home on the south coast to Exmoor over two hundred miles away. It was May and she was due to take part in the fiftieth running of the country's most arduous endurance event for horse and rider, the famous Golden Horseshoe. Her horse, Monty, was already ensconced in the stables there and was settling well. Now she was following his route.

She was thinking that this was the same black strip of tarmac that she and Danny had taken to and from their shopping trips together countless times, carting back their necessities, silly luxuries and occasional treasures. This was the road near which they'd found their dream house seven years ago; the same road they had taken to go to their anniversary celebration fifteen long months ago.

Tonight, though, all those memories led to only one place: her life without Danny.

The setting sun cast its watery rays through the rear window as she steered through the lazy turns hoping to lose those difficult but tenacious thoughts.

"Don't think about it! Look around you," she ordered herself. "Look at the lush green scenery, the slabs of purple clouds hanging over the leaves of the trees; some gold, some burnished deep red. Look at the sunlight, a glowing ribbon draped along the dark belt of pines and oak. Look at the absurd line of cows, walking single file in their spontaneous end of day commute back to the barn. Take in the ghostly white house walls in the small village tucked into the hillside a few miles off the road. And look at you: a thirty-four-year-old woman in a sprightly silver Mazda, driving fast, toward a new life; a life without Danny.

Many miles later she came to a small town and braked for the first of its traffic lights. Her car idled as she selected first gear and held the clutch pedal pressed down.  She mused that neither Danny nor her first driving instructor would have approved and idly glanced to her right. Her heart gave a little thud at what she saw. It was a specialist shop that sold all things marine. She noticed a poster in the window advertising a particular make of boat engine. In this part of the country you couldn't avoid boats. They were in tourist paintings, photos, on mugs, T-shirts, key chains and, of course, there were hundreds of the real things everywhere. There were vessels in their natural habitat on water, as well as on trailers in car parks and trespassing on the road, slowing the passage of lesser vehicles, which had to give way to them even though they were the intruders. What had struck her hard, however, was that the boat pictured in the poster she was now looking at was nearly identical to Danny's. She recognised its size, shape, colour and configuration. He'd bought it about five years ago, and though she thought his interest in it would flag, like that of any boy with a new toy, he'd proved her wrong and spent nearly every weekend on the vessel, fishing like a seasoned professional. He would bring home the best of his catch, which she would clean and cook for their evenings together. Ah, Danny....She swallowed hard and inhaled slowly to calm her pounding heart. It was over a year since he had left and, although she was coping most of the time, she knew she was susceptible to periods of desperation. She had been told that it was normal and that time is a great healer. Well meaning words, but little comfort in her hours of darkness.

The tears began to well and as she fought to regain control she was startled by a honk behind her. The lights had changed to green. The driver behind her became even more impatient when she let the clutch slip and the engine stalled. Her face crimson with embarrassment, she lifted her hand in apology as she eventually managed to move onwards.

She drove on, trying desperately to keep her mind from speculating about his death. She imagined the boat rocking unsteadily in the turbulent grey waters and she pictured him pitch overboard, his arms flailing madly; his panicked voice perhaps crying for help. Oh, my love.....

She cruised through the town's second set of lights and continued toward the coast. In front of her she could see, in the last of the sunlight, the skirt of the Atlantic as it became the Bristol Channel.  To her the water looked menacing, cold and deadly. She had never forgiven the ocean.  She held it to blame for life without Danny. It had become a personal grudge. It was responsible.

Then she told herself: No. Think about Jack instead. Jack Bowen, the man she was about to have dinner with in The Harbour Lights restaurant. It would be the first time she'd been out with a man in a long while.  She'd "met" him online. They'd spoken on the phone a few times and, after considerable skirting around on both their parts, she'd felt comfortable enough to agree to a meeting in person. They'd settled on The Harbour Lights, a popular restaurant on the seafront of the small town. It was many miles from home, but was roughly equidistant for each of them. She knew the place well as she had visited the area with Danny many times. Besides, she was awarding herself a break and intended to drive the short distance from there to The Exmoor White Horse Inn at Exford, where she and Danny had spent blissful days.

Jack had suggested another restaurant which had better food, but she couldn't meet a new man there because it had been one of Danny's favourite places. So The Harbour Lights it was.

She thought back to their phone conversation last night. Jack had said to her, "I'm tall and pretty well built, a little balding on top."

"Okay, well," she'd replied nervously, "I'm five-five, blonde, and I'll be wearing a purple dress."

Sitting in her car, she thought about those words and realised how that simple exchange typified single life, meeting people you'd "met" only over the phone or via a computer. She had no problem with dating. In fact she was looking forward to it in a way. She'd met her husband when he was just graduating from university and she was twenty-one. They'd become engaged almost immediately and that had been the end of her social life as a single woman. But now she'd have some fun. She'd meet interesting men; she'd begin to enjoy sex again.

Even if it was work at first, she'd try to just relax. She'd try not to be bitter, try not to be too much of a widow. But even as she was thinking this her thoughts went somewhere else. Would she ever actually fall in *love* again? The way she'd once been so completely in love with Danny? And would anybody love *her* completely?

At another red light Lisa reached up and twisted the mirror toward her, glancing into it. The sun was now below the horizon and the light was dim but she believed she passed the rear view mirror test with flying colours. She saw full lips, a face devoid of wrinkles which was reminiscent of a young film star (albeit in a poorly lit Mazda's mirror) and a petite nose. Then, too, her body was slim and pretty firm, and though she knew her breasts wouldn't land her on the cover of a magazine, she had a feeling that in a pair of nice tight jeans, she would draw some serious attention. She was still fragile, but was trying to be positive. She told herself, she'd find a man who was right for her; somebody who could appreciate the young woman within her, the woman who could ride a horse with the best of them. Or maybe she'd find somebody who'd love her academic side; her writing and poetry and her love of life, or somebody who could laugh with her at movies, at funny jokes and dumb ones. How she loved laughing, and how little of it she'd done lately. Then Lisa Richards thought: No, wait, wait ... she'd find a man who loved *everything* about her.

But then the tears started and she pulled off the road quickly, surrendering to the sobs. 'No, no, no ...She forced the images of her husband out of her mind. The cold water, the grey water ...

Five minutes later she'd calmed down, wiped her eyes dry and reapplied her makeup and lipstick. She'd had a long drive. It was the first time she had ever driven so far, with or without Danny by her side and she was pleased with her achievement. She parked next to the restaurant and glanced at her car clock, which told her it was just five o'clock. She had deliberately made sure of being early. She wanted to park in a convenient spot and be ready to get away if necessary. Jack Bowen had told her that he'd be unable to meet her until six- thirty, so she had an hour and a half to get used to her surroundings. She walked slowly through the small town, taking in its sights and sounds and peering through its shop windows. On a whim she treated herself to some risqué lingerie, wondering as soon as she left the shop whether anybody would ever see her in it.

She sat on a bench close to a small marina to gather herself. Lisa watched a couple sitting in the stern of their boat, glasses half empty, flirting without a care in the world. She saw them laughing and talking before draining their glasses and disappearing out of sight into the cabin. She was lost in thought but her reverie was disturbed as for the second time that day she jumped at the sound of a car horn and for the second time crimson flooded her cheeks. The passing male driver turned his head to further appreciate the view but had gone before she was able locate him. She smiled to herself at the compliment and ran her fingers over the bag containing the lingerie.  There was a noticeable lightness, almost a girlish skip, as she retraced her steps to arrive at the restaurant a full thirty minutes early.

She wondered uneasily if it would be all right if she sat in the bar by herself and had a glass of wine. She admonished herself inwardly and told herself she could do anything she wanted. This was *her* night.

-8-

A mere three miles away from the Harbour Lights restaurant, Quentin Legard walked up the drive of a substantial detached property. The lawn to his right was cut meticulously and the flower beds to his left bore testament to the gardener's attention to detail and many hours of hard work. He carried a small black bag and there was an ID badge hanging from a chain around his neck. As he neared the front door he could see lights within and one or two windows were slightly open, allowing a cooling breeze to waft inside. He glanced at his watch, rang the bell and the door opened before the echo had even faded.

Before him stood a pretty woman in her late thirties. She was thin and her hair was dark and untidy in an attractive way. She wore an expensive white blouse which was not tucked into her designer jeans. He couldn't help noticing that she smelled of alcohol.

"Yes?"

"I'm from your phone company," said Quentin, holding out his ID as proof. "We're checking the broadband connections in the area and I need to make sure yours are working properly."

The woman blinked, trying to focus and take in the information, but she couldn't see his name.

"The broadband? Well, it has been a bit slow lately and we pay so much for it."

"That's why we need to check it, madam," purred Quentin.

"I was using it earlier and it took ages to download something," she ventured.

"Well, that means it definitely needs some attention, madam. In fact, we've had to fix quite a few in this road already," Quentin pressed on. "Of course, if it's not convenient I can always get the office to phone and make another appointment, but it would be several weeks away, I'm afraid."

The woman missed the obvious fact that Quentin's visit was not a pre-arranged appointment in the first place.

"How long will it take?" she asked.

"Not long; perhaps ten minutes," replied Quentin.

"Ok as long as it's not much longer. Fancy a drink, I'm having one?" she said.

"Love one, but I'm not allowed during working hours," he replied.

He followed appreciatively as she showed him through the house, sipping as she went.  He bent over the phone connection boxes in each room for a short while, before indicating he was ready for the next. When the downstairs had been dealt with he followed her up the stairs as she swayed in front of him. She paused at the top of the landing and checked over her shoulder to ensure he was there.

This is a big house to be on your own," he fished.

"Yes it is," she turned to look directly at him, "it can get very lonely."

Quentin Legard was on a tight schedule as he had another job across town at 6.30.

He sighed as he considered the situation.

"So," he asked, "are there any more I need to look at?"

"Just one," she replied and moved towards her bedroom. "Follow me."

She sat on the unmade bed as he crouched over the phone terminal by the bed side.  He lingered over this last one for a while before rising.  He turned to face the woman.

"Could you do me a favour?" he asked. "Check this socket to make sure it's working properly; it's the key to the rest of the house. Then I'll need your signature to say you're satisfied."

"Ok," she said and bent forward to concentrate.

She felt very little as Quentin Legard slipped his thin cord over her head from behind and pulled it into a noose.  He tightened the garrotte by turning the screwdriver that he had looped through it. A few turns later and she had ceased struggling; her body limp. He dragged her off the bed and laid her on the floor.  He had not even broken sweat. He listened carefully and checked the front of the house through the window. All was quiet and undisturbed. He lifted his sleeve to look at his watch and was more than disappointed to note the time. He would not be able to complete his task and made a mental note to himself to plan more carefully next time.

He slipped out of the house, walked back down the drive and settled himself into his car.  He removed the latex gloves and wondered whether the tipsy woman had even noticed them.  As he started the engine he brought to the front of his mind the name he had given for the evening appointment.

"So, Jack Bowen, let's see what tonight brings," he whispered to himself as looked at his ID card.  He had made sure his thumb had covered his name when he had shown it to the woman. He calmly coaxed the vehicle towards The Harbour Lights restaurant.

-9-

She didn't notice him enter the restaurant, but spotted his cheery wave from across the room as he approached her at the bar.  She waved back and took him in.  She saw a good-looking man in a dark suit and she was pleased to note that he wore no tie as it would have been out of place.  He was obviously well muscled and carried himself with an easy confidence. She liked what she saw. The slightly balding feature didn't register and wouldn't have mattered anyway.

"Lisa? I'm Jack," he introduced himself with a firm hand and she reciprocated, wanting also to appear relaxed and in control of herself.

He sat on the stool next to her at the bar and ordered sparkling water.  Lisa declined his offer of more wine.

"I hope I haven't kept you waiting too long," he said, "I got held up at my last appointment."

"No, I've only just got here myself.  I took the opportunity of getting some fresh air in town."

They chatted for a few minutes and were then called to their table.  It looked out of the window at the marina and the twinkling lights were already taking over from the fading sunlight. The water had become a menacing grey and Lisa could see that people were putting on warmer clothes as they walked past. First meetings are never easy and uncomfortable silences can develop as each person decides what to say and is conscious of the impression being made. They made small talk about the weather and the national news.  Eventually Jack volunteered that he was divorced, had no children and regretted that hole in his life. Lisa told him that she and Danny had not had children either, but she wasn't sure whether or not she wanted any. She told him about her horse and the forthcoming event on Exmoor, but fell short of saying that she was heading there that night after their dinner. She felt she was being as adventurous as she dared.

"I see you've been shopping," he said, indicating the bag tucked under the table by her feet.

"Yes, I thought I'd treat myself for a change," she blushed as the words left her lips.

He was polite enough not to pursue it.

The meal went well and they warmed to each other as time passed.

"Let's go outside," he suggested.

Lisa was unsure, but knew she was at a crossroads. She'd had thoughts about such an evening so many times.  This was what her life should be like.  A good restaurant, a meal, the marina, the emerging stars, the twinkling lights of the boats in the marina; all shared with a handsome man. They strolled until they came to the bench she had occupied earlier. As he sat down his jacket opened slightly, to reveal a thin cord almost escaping from an inside pocket.

"You're going to lose something," she said, indicating the cord.

He glanced down and frowned. "Thanks," he said, "a necessary item, I'm afraid. I use it quite often." He tucked it away.

They sat in silence for some time and words became difficult. Just as she was about to break the ice again, the amorous couple re-appeared on the rear of their boat.

"Is that him?" Jack Bowen asked, nodding to the front.

"Yes," said Lisa. "That's my husband. That's Danny." She shivered with disgust as she watched him kiss the woman with him. At that precise moment a cold wind blew all her dreams away.  "When's it going to happen?" she asked, her voice betraying her fear.

"Let's walk," he replied, "It's getting chilly. I've seen enough and so have you, I think."

They walked slowly away from the marina and he made sure there was nobody within hearing distance before he gave his answer.

"It depends. Who's the woman with him?"

"I've never seen her before," Lisa replied. "I expect it's just one of the many he brings to his boat every weekend.  There must have been so many." There were tears in her eyes now and she fought to hold them back.

"Will she be there all night?" Jack asked.

"'No. I've been spying on him for a month. He'll kick her out around midnight and there'll be another one tomorrow." Lisa managed to say through tightly pursed lips.

Jack nodded. "Then it's tonight. After he's asleep I'll get on board, tie him up and take the boat out a few miles.  It will look like he was drunk and got tangled in the anchor line and went overboard. I'll take the boat to the next town, grab a small dinghy and get back in.  The boat will be left just drifting, so it will look like an accident."

"Do you always make it look like an accident?" Lisa wondered whether she had asked one question too many and broken the hit man's code.

"As often as I can," he replied. "I mentioned the job I did earlier this afternoon. It was all about a woman who had been abusing her children.  The husband couldn't get the children to say anything to the police. They didn't want to get her into trouble so the husband hired me.  I made it look like a failed rape attempt."

"God, how awful," Lisa was incredulous. She looked at him in a fresh light. "Aren't you worried I might be a policewoman or something?"

Jack Bowen laughed in response. "No, I've been checking you out online ever since you contacted me. You're exactly who you say you are. A woman hiring a professional hit on her husband for twenty five thousand pounds."

"Speaking of which," Lisa said as she pulled a thick envelope from her handbag and handed it to him. It disappeared rapidly into the same pocket as the thin cord. "Will he feel anything?" she asked.

"No," he replied, "the water's so cold he'll pass out before he drowns."

Lisa Richards gave it some consideration before her reply. "That's a shame."

They had been walking slowly absorbed in concentration and had reached the end of the marina road.

"You are sure you want this done?" Jack asked, seeking confirmation.

"Oh I'm sure," she said through gritted teeth. "The man who tells me he goes fishing every weekend and spends the time with who knows how many other women; the man who announces he doesn't want children even though we agreed we did; the man who treats me like a chattel, a slave; the man who has the audacity to calmly come back with the fish he says he's caught for me to cook after having spent the weekend doing his own version of fishing all weekend, deserves what's coming his way." She surprised both herself and Jack with the calm, measured strength of her answer. It allowed no room for doubt.

Quentin Legard, known on this occasion as Jack Bowen, shook her hand. "I'll take care of things," he said, "you practice playing the grieving widow."

"That will be easy," she said, "I've been the grieving wife for years."

Pulling her coat collar up high, she returned to her car, not looking back at either her husband or the man who was about to kill him. She climbed into her Mazda, started the engine and played her favourite music very loud. She held the electric window button down on her side until the car filled with the sharp May air as she drove as fast as she dared away from her previous existence towards her future. She pointed the car towards Exmoor and wondered what life held for her there in the next few days. At the very least she would be busy with the Golden Horseshoe competition, which would take her mind off recent events.

## KEVIN AND KAREN WILSON

### -10-

Six months before Lisa Richards concluded her business with the man she knew as Jack Bowen, Kevin and Karen Wilson were finishing their evening meal and lingering over coffee and mints. They had deliberately taken their meal slowly for this was a special night. The Exmoor White Horse Inn is rightly proud of its food, and the chef had excelled himself that night.  Kevin had secretly arranged the menu when he had made the booking.  He had also deliberately booked them into one of the rooms in the adjoining lodge, because it has the benefit of being larger than most others and there is a private garden with its own access to the gently babbling River Exe as it tumbles from the moor before gathering pace and volume on its journey down the valley that bears its name. All he needed was for the sun to shine and a greater being than he had arranged for that week in November to bless them both.

They had spent the day exploring the vicinity and making arrangements for Karen's horse to be stabled next to the inn. Karen was due to compete in the fiftieth running of the Golden Horseshoe the following May, and she was nervously looking forward to the challenge. They had many friends, colleagues, contacts and family members who had pledged not inconsiderable sums of money to sponsor her in the event.  These preparations were not, however, the only reason for them being there. They were not even the main reason.

Kevin had trained to teach at St Paul's College, Cheltenham, and he and his friends, like many students devoid of parental oversight and other controls, were prone to many excesses. Sometimes, spurred on by a particularly bad hangover or a disastrous sexual encounter, they used to declare that they were 'going halibut', which was their play on the phrase 'going celibate'. As young, healthy men none of them ever gave up their vices for very long, and Kevin was no different.  Little did he imagine that less than 40 years later, he'd find himself forced into 'going halibut' again as he fought prostate cancer.

His cancer was picked up by chance when he went to his GP for a minor matter.  He suggested that Kevin was due a 'mid-life MOT', so all the usual things were checked: cholesterol levels, blood pressure and prostate cancer susceptibility. Kevin thought it was a formality and was unconcerned. As a sports teacher and regular gym-goer, he was pretty fit and never ill. He was 6 feet tall and at 17 stone probably overweight, but put that down to having been a prop forward.  A week later, he was called in to the surgery to discuss an anomaly on the PSA (Prostate Specific Antigen) result. He knew this test could indicate the presence of prostate cancer but it never occurred to him that he might be at risk. Further tests over the next few weeks confirmed that he did indeed have prostate cancer and it was at an advanced stage. To say it shook Kevin is an understatement as he'd had no symptoms. His 81-year-old father had been diagnosed with prostate cancer four years previously and was told that he would die of old age before the cancer got him. Even then Kevin had never considered himself at risk.  But, as he discovered, younger men do get prostate cancer, and the cancer 'feeds' off the male hormone testosterone, so it's so important to act fast. What happened next was like a whirlwind that blew him and his family away. Events became uncontrollable and he was scheduled for immediate surgery.

They both knew that he could be left impotent after the operation and had argued with the doctors, insisting they needed the few days on Exmoor to come to terms with the devastation to their lives. It was their way of trying to cope. They wanted to share what they feared might be an idyllic finale. That night they made love knowing that it could be the last time. It was tender, slow, beautiful and hugely meaningful, being based on their deep love for each other and the circumstances in which they found themselves. Afterwards Kevin jokingly shook his wife's hands and thanked her for a wonderful sex life during their 32 years of marriage. It caused them to laugh as they lay in each other's arms, but soon unstoppable tears traced rivulets down their cheeks and soaked the pillows. They held each other tightly as both somehow realised it had been the last time and another phase in their life together was beginning.

His joke had been prophetic. It was the calm before the storm.

Kevin underwent surgery for a radical prostatectomy to remove the prostate gland and tissue around it on New Year's Eve. That was a great irony to him as he knew everyone else in the world was having a great time while he was being cut in two. The only upside was the fact that he felt little pain, even though he now had a scar that ran from his navel to his pubic bone. He called it one of the "Nasties." There were other nasties to deal with, however.

What few men appreciate is how emasculating the treatment can be. He found having a catheter fitted, while his wounds healed, demeaning. His father tried to console him with the observation that people would get used to smelling him before they saw him. Humour can be a great comfort but those six weeks were trying. For a start, it meant he couldn't sleep in the same bed as Karen because the bag was cumbersome and it was difficult to move about. Then there was the time it burst and leaked on the floor, not to mention what it felt like to have the thing taken out. Another of the less glorious experiences of those few months was the nappy pads. He had to wear them post catheter for about a month, until he regained control of his bladder, and he was conscious of every sneeze. He religiously did the prescribed pelvic floor exercises to strengthen the muscles supporting the bladder.

He had a course of radiotherapy, which finished two days before his 54th birthday. One additional bugbear was that he had to take the female hormone oestrogen to cut down his testosterone levels. This, he was told, might mean he would put weight on around the middle, which proved to be correct. He knew it could also make his breasts grow a little and leave them feeling tender. He thought to himself, in another moment of humour, that if that happened he would feel like every middle-aged woman in the country. In addition, he started to experience a burning sensation in his waterworks. At first, he thought he must have a bladder infection but after a course of antibiotics failed to help, he did some research on the internet and concluded it was radiation cystitis. As one nurse put it, it's like sunburn on the inside caused by the radiotherapy. Drinking lots of water helped, but it was yet another nasty.

Before the operation, Kevin and Karen talked long and hard about all the possible side effects. The worst, they knew, was the risk of impotence as approximately ten per cent of men are left impotent after treatment. As it turned out, the surgeon needed to excise a wider area than expected because the prostate had fused to his bladder and rectum so the nerve damage was unavoidable and could not be reversed. This had an effect on their marital physical activities.  Kevin and Karen were told that he could have an implant, which may be pumped up at the relevant moment, but to them it seemed hugely comedic.

With massive courage they decided it would have to mean the end of their physical relationship.  They had no regrets, however, because they shared intimate and extraordinary memories. They reasoned that staying alive was a far more important goal.

Kevin knew he was not out of the woods yet. Consultants don't like to give figures but when he pressed for one, on the basis that this was, after all, his life, he was told that he had between three to ten years. There are four grades of cancer from T1 to T4 - with T4 being the worst. His was on the cusp of T3 and T4 which means that it was almost certain that the cancer would reappear somewhere else.

Although an optimistic person by nature, he inevitably had moments of great melancholy. Certain songs, such as Father and Daughter, by Paul Simon set him thinking about their daughter, whilst others brought his son to mind. He found it hard to tell them that he was seriously ill, so he restricted himself to the facts.  As the man of the house he felt responsible for them both, and he hoped that he had taught them all he could and had been a good father and husband. Kevin knew the love he felt for them transcended this life and held onto that with pride in his darkest moments.

His work colleagues were always on hand and he became quite emotional when he thought about how supportive everyone had been.  Karen joked that it was the effect of the female hormones. She and Kevin found themselves kissing and holding hands more than ever and there was a new tenderness in their relationship.

The local newspaper ran an article on their story, as did the local radio station.  Kevin's philosophy was to be perfectly honest and hide nothing.  He had been a hard, no nonsense rugby player and he dealt with his situation in the same way, even though it had highlighted many inner fears and he was scared. The following is a transcript of one of his interviews:

*"Coping with impotence, whether temporarily, or as in my case, permanently, is one of the many consequences of this disease which is rarely talked about. I don't suppose any of my friends will have even thought about it, so that's why I have decided to speak out in the hope that other men my age will realise the dangers and seek early detection.*

*So what does the future hold?  For me: regular blood tests. The cancer had spread to my lymph nodes, which gives a difficult prognosis as the lymph system runs through the body and the cancer could be transported elsewhere. Meanwhile, spurred on by my diagnosis, a few weeks ago, my college friends and I met up for a reunion. The first thing I did was tell everyone to get checked up right away. Many of them have done so and as this is a familial disease, so has my brother, who is 50. He lives in the North West and initially, when he went to his GP and asked for a PSA test, he* was told he couldn't have one as he 'had no symptoms and the test was not accurate'. He went back, on my advice, to demand the test and thankfully, was in the clear. But it goes to show that the postcode lottery is real, so don't accept no for an answer.

Where I live there is a high detection and cure rate for prostate cancer because GPs are choosing to be vigilant, but this is not the case everywhere, so I implore every man with a familial history of prostate cancer, and any man aged 50 or more, to demand a PSA test and physical examination. If you are not prepared to do it for yourself, then do it for your family's sake. This disease is curable when caught early. Why would you choose not to give yourself and your family a better chance? We men are not good at facing our fears but, as I have learnt, there are some things we need to talk about so we can fight them head on. It may be that in the near future, I will have to face some bad news. But I am not going to worry until it happens, and hopefully it won't. In the meantime, I am going to focus on getting on with my life."

The newspapers and radio also mentioned that Kevin and Karen had set up a fund, which they jokingly called "Balls to Cancer." Karen's entry into the Golden Horseshoe was specifically to raise money for the fund and Kevin and a couple of his rugby playing friends were due to act as her support team.  There would be no more committed team in the event.

## THE EVENING BEFORE

### -11-

The organisers of The Golden Horseshoe held a briefing for all competitors in the Function Room at The White Horse during the afternoon before the event.  Details of classes, routes, rules, timetables, health and safety, support team procedures, veterinary arrangements and prizes were made clear. There was also feedback from previous events.

A rider from a previous year, Tamsyn Carter, gave a personal account as she tackled the Exmoor challenge, with her horse, Dobbin. She stood at the front of the room and recounted her experience.

"Given the weather I must say actually going to a major ride was a massive plus.  It had been so wet that the venue owner only allowed us to go ahead, provided no lorries went on the field. In fact, up until 3 days beforehand we still were not sure if we were going.  I'm sure I was not alone in praying that all our training would not be wasted.

Well, what a ride! Previously I had only done the 40-40 class 3 years ago and then only very slowly. We have some very small hills in Hertfordshire, and there are no gates or fords where I live.

Although I have been riding since I was a young girl this was my greatest challenge on a horse. I'm not very comfortable with heights, so didn't know what to expect. Some of you sensible people out there (I know there are some) may say I was potentially biting off more than I could chew by entering the 120K. However, I had my secret weapon: my daughter Katie to help with training and my horse Dobbin. Thankfully they are with me again this year.

I don't want to do a normal ride report as I am sure you will see one of those elsewhere, but here are just a few main points of interest from my experience:

Exmoor has very variable weather! On the top of the Moor it was about 4 degrees with a wind-chill down to goodness knows what. We had horizontal stinging hail at one point. You know it's cold when you are approaching crew cars and they are all sitting inside shivering! Meanwhile in the valleys it was warm and humid. I had to do a spider-man at one crew stop: I had to jump off and strip off a couple of layers.

My mobile signal was very patchy and I don't think it will have improved this year.

Shaving your legs is very important!  I know it's not meant to be a fashion parade but Katie gave me some stick on padding to help prevent shin bruising. Ladies...I don't think I need to explain the problem: ouch!

I think it's important to look out for your fellow riders and help them if necessary. I was helped by a kind man, whose name I still don't know, who very kindly jumped off his horse to lead it through a ford that Dobbin had decided was unsuitable and so set his off as well. I felt very guilty as I had long waterproof boots on while he was in trainers: I wish he had told me he was about to do that as I could have braved the ice cold water! My knight in shining armour!

Not wishing to be over-dramatic but doing this ride really is very tough, especially on the horse. I went too fast at the start on the first (80K) day and ended up leading Dobbin up the last mile of a very steep hill up to the venue....my mistake that cost me a gold award but I learnt my lesson on pacing and he sailed around the 40K on the second day. As we trotted up to the last two grass fields he saw the end and I said "do you want to canter then?" He powered up to the finish. Handy hint for spectators at the massive wooden horseshoe marking the end: don't assume horses will stop! Thankfully, Dobbin did.

For any of you who would like to do this ride: and I can honestly say it was a FANTASTIC achievement. I am still so proud of Dobbin that I get a tear in my eye just thinking about it. The scenery, camaraderie and organisation are second to none so I'd urge anyone to have a go, but I hope you've trained for it."

Tamsyn sat down to a round of applause, wondering what the next few days held for her. Karen and Kevin sat through the session, taking it all in. He held her hand throughout and took pride in the fact that his wife was taking part in the face of such a crisis for the couple. From what he heard he felt confident that they were as well prepared as possible and he knew he could rely on the support team they had with them. Lisa Richards missed the session because she was still concluding her business with the man she knew as Jack Bowen. The party from America spent the afternoon on a trip and returned to the inn with barely enough time to change for the evening meal. The Honeymoon Suite couple spent the afternoon in their room, having had a delicious cream tea for lunch outside by the river. They did not spend the time sleeping.

Quentin Legard also missed the briefing. He had not intended being there at all, but he had no other contracts for the next two weeks and, more significantly, he couldn't resist the temptation of seeing Lisa again. After all, she was a single woman now. He had concluded his business with Lisa Richards' husband and arrived at the inn in the early hours of the next morning, having been fortunate in securing a room via a cancellation. He had, in fact, been delayed by an unplanned event and there was nothing he disliked more than an unplanned event.  It offended his sense of order and in his line of work the unexpected normally meant problems.  Nevertheless, he had dealt with it efficiently and was pleased with the outcome. He now lay in bed scanning the list of competitors and his interest was piqued by the fact that they were predominantly women.  Plenty of scope, he thought as he turned out the light.  He knew he would sleep as he always had: untroubled by conscience and totally untouched by guilt.

Earlier, the briefing for The Golden Horseshoe had ended with the organiser lifting a bag from the floor and placing it on the table in front of her. With an exaggerated flourish she pulled an object from the bag and held it up for all to see.

"Ladies and Gentlemen," she trilled, "we are proud to announce that as this year is the fiftieth running of The Golden Horseshoe Challenge there will be a special award.  The judges will decide which horse and rider is to receive this magnificent trophy." There was an audible gasp as all eyes became riveted on a gold horseshoe. "This trophy is actually hallmarked gold. It is not plated and has been specially handcrafted for our special occasion.  We would like to thank the various sponsors who have donated in order to make this possible. It is a truly a spectacular prize. The judges' decision will be final, but I can assure you they will be considering everything that happens over the next two days. In fact they have already begun their deliberations by inspecting everybody's applications and their details. I will not introduce the judges because they wish to remain anonymous and impartial. That way none of you can bribe them at the bar or anything. You may therefore be assured that whoever wins this, it will be utterly deserved. The organising committee would like to thank everybody who has helped to put on the challenge for this special year and we wish all of you the very best of luck.  We have left nothing to chance, and neither, I hope, have you. The only thing out of our control is the weather and I hope the gods of Exmoor are looking at us with kindly eyes. You all have your own start times, so have a good evening and we'll see you there tomorrow."

Nobody noticed the two men from Manchester standing at the back of the room, taking it all in without comment. As the meeting ended they spirited themselves away and headed for the bar.

-12-

At about six o'clock, just as the briefing was finishing, David Trent, the man from the Honeymoon Suite, took his customary place on a bar stool. He had enjoyed his afternoon and had lingered long in the shower before shaving and dressing smartly, but comfortably, for dinner.  His wife, Mary, would join him in one hour, as was her routine.  He was greeted by the owner of the inn and they shook hands firmly; old friends picking up with mutual warmth.

"Good to see you again, I hope all is well with you and your good lady," Peter welcomed him.

"Likewise," replied David, "and I trust the family are well?"

"Very good, thank you," Peter replied. "Linda will be here in a minute."

"Good, I like to say hello when we're here.  Could I have my usual whisky, please?  Glenturret."

Peter disappeared for a few moments and, as if by magic, a large malt whisky was placed on the bar. David took a long appreciative sip, savoured the warmth and depth of flavour and swallowed the nectar.

"Wonderful!" He pronounced.

He asked for the wine list and carefully chose a fine red wine to accompany their evening meal.  Peter, ever the professional and accommodating host, uncorked the bottle and placed it on their favourite table in the restaurant, there to breathe for almost an hour. David had never understood why people had wine uncorked at the table so that it was tasted and consumed before its optimum condition was reached.

David cast his eyes around the room and took it all in.  The place was already working its magic as he felt the calm enveloping him like a familiar and very welcome comfort blanket. The ambience, the sincerity of the owners, the location, the good whisky and the promise of fine food had never failed. The bar gradually filled and the buzz of relaxed conversation filled the air.

"Hello," said the man, who was waiting to be served and had obviously visited the bar on more than one occasion already. "The name's Brian," he stated.

David regarded the figure. The man was somewhat overweight, a fact exaggerated by his diminutive stature. To David, he appeared almost as round as he was tall. His trousers were baggy and not coping with his expanding waistline.  He wore a checked shirt, which stressed his lack of stature, and which was winning its battle to escape the restrictions of a tightly pulled leather belt. His face was also rotund and its colour reflected the alcoholic abuse to which his body had been subjected on a long term basis. The hair on his head was obviously giving up the fight and had retreated to form an almost perfectly symmetrical horseshoe. It was golden in colour and, even under the less than harsh light in the bar, his dome shone brightly like a permanently lit orange beacon. The overall effect was comic to say the least.

"Hello," said David, more from the need for civility than from an interest in continuing any conversation. "Are you here for the Golden Horseshoe?" He asked with a smile, as the comparison between the man's hair and the forthcoming equine competition came to the forefront of his mind.

"God no!" answered Brian, "I wouldn't be seen dead on a horse. Vile things, but don't say that too loudly round here. I'm a property developer. I live in the village. I have a few places I rent out when the competition is on, so I'm not totally against it all."

"That's nice," David said, because he couldn't think of a suitable response.

"Actually," said Brian, seemingly intent on pursuing the conversation with his newly found friend, "I'm making a killing this week.  These horsey types will pay anything to be here, so who am I to miss out?"

"That's nice," repeated David.

Brian missed the sarcasm and ploughed on. "What's your line of work?" he asked."

"Oh, I'm retired. We're just here for a break for a few days," answered David, determined not to reveal details about his background and trying to end the exchange.  Also, his glass was empty and he wanted to order a refill.

"Here; let me," said Brian as he caught the barman's attention. "The usual for me and whatever my friend here is drinking."

David did not like being regarded as this man's friend. "No, I couldn't.  I'm only having this one and then we're due in for dinner," he said.

Brian was not taking no for an answer. "I insist; after all, between you and me, I can claim it on expenses as a business meeting.  The taxman never checks up."

"Surely, that's not right," said David. "If everybody paid the taxes they should, we wouldn't have any trouble funding our schools and health service.  Besides, what about fairness?"

"Everybody does it, so it is fair!" exclaimed Brian, becoming somewhat boastful as he warmed to his pet subject. "Only idiots declare everything. In fact, between you and me again, there's lots I don't declare.  Nobody knows, so why worry? I don't declare my rental income and I claim all the expenses I can. I mean, what are the chances they are going to check up on me?"

David thought they might be quite good if he continued in such a loud and boastful manner, but remained silent and quietly drank from his newly delivered glass, looking directly at the man. He made a decision.

"Actually, a friend of mine might be looking for a place to rent. Have you got a card or something?" said David.

"Of course," the man replied, his bald pate by now glistening as the heat in the room took effect. He handed his business card to David. "I've got four places I rent out, and three more being built now.  They're almost finished, so I might even retire like you and let the money roll in!" He laughed at his own joke, but David didn't join in.

"Can I get him to call you?" asked David. "I'll tell him we met here and you gave me your details.

"Of course," Brian replied, "no problem. I look forward to hearing from him."

"Excellent," David said. "Now, if you'll excuse me, I have to go to the dining room to check on something. It was nice meeting you."

He slipped from the stool, turned his back on his unwelcome acquaintance, and walked towards the restaurant. He was met by the sight of one of the waitresses. Dressed in black she was smart and trim. She greeted him as an old friend. They hugged as he kissed her on both cheeks and she blushed demurely as they both lingered and held the clinch.

"Welcome back," she said.

"It's good to be back," he replied and to see you again. "How are you?"

"Great," she said, "all the better now. Is your wife well?"

He knew her enquiry was genuine. "She's fine. We'll be in soon for dinner. I just came in to check the wine was on the table and breathing."

"It certainly is," she said. "Peter gave it to me and I put it there myself. I knew it was for you, so I made sure everything is as you like it."

"Thank you," David said. "I hope you're doing our table this evening."

"Of course," she replied. "That was never in doubt. Look forward to seeing you a bit later."

They parted company with another hug and David strolled back to the bar. He was pleased to note that Brian was nowhere to be seen as he eased himself onto the bar stool again.

Peter appeared and set another drink on the bar.

"On the house," he said. "Sorry about Brian, but I was busy and couldn't get here in time to stop him."

"Thank you. That's fine, don't worry," David replied. "It was all a bit one sided. I've always found it odd that some people can't help themselves. They just don't listen to answers to their questions. He didn't seem to want to wait for any reply I gave. I don't think he noticed that I didn't tell him I worked for HMRC before I retired."

Peter raised his eyes to the ceiling, smiled, and moved along the bar to serve another customer.

At the other end of the bar another local man stood clutching his pint. There was a twinkle in his eye as he engaged Peter.

"So, what's with the buckets?" he asked.

"I don't know what you mean," replied Peter, even though he knew full well.

"A man works hard all day, has a drink at this posh place on the way home and has to piss in a bucket! It's like going camping. What's going on? It's not exactly what you expect, is it? " he exclaimed.

"It's good, isn't it?" replied Peter. "We thought we'd bring some culture into your life."

"Culture? What's cultured about that?" continued the local man, laughing good-naturedly.

"We thought there might be some chance of you actually aiming straight," responded Peter, "rather than taking your usual guess about it."

David listened to the exchange and laughed with the two men. Linda, Peter's wife, appeared at David's side.

"Hello again," she said and they greeted each other with a mutual kiss on the cheek. "Good to see you."

"Hello," replied David.  "I was just listening to Peter having his ear bent about the buckets. What's that all about?

Linda laughed.  "That's my fault," she said. "We needed to refurbish the toilets for men and women.  I got a designer in and she came up with the idea of three buckets instead of the usual arrangement. They look cleaner, don't make as much mess and you men need something bigger to aim at. Peter just left it to me, so that's we got. It's novel isn't it? It's caused quite a stir, I can tell you."

"I bet it has," said David, laughing with Linda. "Stay here, I'll try them out."

David returned a few minutes later, sporting a broad grin. As he passed the complaining local man, he said "I don't know what the problem is. I like the buckets. Linda's done a good job there."

The man heard the comment and looked across at Linda with a bemused expression.

"It always takes a woman to understand what a man needs," she said with finality. "I'd be glad to help if it's too difficult for you. Perhaps you'd like a personal lesson?

"I just do as I'm told," Peter put in, avoiding the man's gaze by pulling a pint for another customer.

"What's been done for the ladies?" asked David.

"Don't even go there," advised Peter as Linda slipped from the room.

-13-

The meeting finished in good time for people to adjourn to the bar and then to enjoy a leisurely evening meal. The bar was buzzing and the restaurant was fully booked. The Manchester men, Dennis and Vince, stood centrally at the bar. At one end they noticed a middle aged man, sitting on a stool sipping whisky and chatting to the landlord, whilst at the other extreme a smiling local with a glint in his eye stood with his pint. The Golden Horseshoe organiser and her entourage swept in and sat at the nearest available table. The formidable lady wrestled her bag into position underneath and clamped her legs into position around it. Dennis wondered to himself whether the golden prize was still contained therein, whilst Vince mused that the woman's legs were probably plenty strong enough to prevent invasion, but he worried about damage to the golden horseshoe. He remembered that he had once dated a horse loving woman and her thighs, though having a thousand tales to tell, damn near finished him off. It was not a mistake he was likely to repeat, he vowed. From then on he had stuck to night clubs and discos, but even then his experiences had been pretty hairy at times and on one occasion that description had turned out to be accurate, much to his shock and disbelief. He took a sip of his drink and tried to banish the memory.

The pair listened to the banter around them and tried to become part of the scenery. They were used to sitting unnoticed whenever they were away from home, and had developed the skill of homing in on anything that caught their attention. That evening, much of the talk concerned a spate of robberies from local farms. Quad Bikes and other machinery had been stolen and the victims were not backward in voicing their opinions about what they would do to the thieves if they caught them. The police were obviously involved, but the Exmoor community were also actively searching. Nothing had yet been recovered and nobody in particular appeared to be on their lips as suspects. One interesting fact they did overhear was that some locals had grouped together and hired a private contractor to find the perpetrators and, hopefully, recover their valuable assets. It was no business of theirs but the pair made a mental note. They had long ago learned that sometimes seemingly innocuous things can become important and useful.

Dennis and Vince did not wish to be noticed and avoided eye contact for fear of being engaged in conversation. Neither was married. Dennis, however, was due to tie the knot later that summer for his second attempt at marital bliss. Vince was solidly single and had been that way since his marriage had collapsed amid a flurry of acrimony and a torrent of incomprehensible paperwork, the effect of which was to significantly reduce his bank balance.

They were in business together, or more accurately, Vince worked for Dennis as a sub contractor.  Both were trained electricians and had been working at Manchester Airport doing maintenance when Dennis was approached by an acquaintance about installing heating systems in churches. After much careful research they realised that there were at that time very few companies in the market. Under-pew electric heating seemed to be all the rage and as congregations were growing older they needed warmth in order to persuade them to continue attending. This, combined with the fact that people are now used to, and expect, central heating convinced the men that a joint venture could well succeed. They had not been wrong.  One drawback was the time spent away from home, but the rewards were great. Churches are not easy institutions to deal with, but they rapidly developed a reputation based on word of mouth recommendation, which is the best kind of advertising. They were now in a position to pick and choose their work and were able to stay in better places when they were away. They were at Exford to install heating in a nearby church on Exmoor and were due to take five days completing the work.

Unfortunately, they were both prone to lapses of judgement in other matters.  Vince's weakness was his choice of female companions, so he had little cash, whilst Dennis was constantly seeking opportunities of making money. He had already made enough to purchase a property in Florida, and was looking to the day when he no longer needed to work. It was a lethal combination and the sight of the golden horseshoe sent both brains into overdrive. They concluded that to forego such a heaven sent opportunity would be a criminal waste.

Having ordered a second pint they managed to fend off competition for seats at a table from a short, rather rotund character, who had a strikingly shiny dome circled by a ring of hair, which was withdrawing its services in the face of a superior force. This gave them a better view of their surroundings and the other people there. They watched as the defeated man shrugged his shoulders in acceptance and turned his attention to engaging somebody else in conversation. He tried several people before approaching a middle aged man sitting on his own at the end of the bar minding his own business, enjoying his glass of whisky. That man had been talking to the landlord when he was interrupted by the short character. Dennis noticed that, although polite to the newcomer, the attention was obviously not welcome. As they watched the unfolding scene, the short man grew more and more animated; using his hands and arms to stress the points he was making.  Unfortunately, they couldn't eavesdrop as the general buzz was too loud, but it became obvious that he was a boastful character and his acquaintance was finding him tiresome.

Vince nodded towards the bar and asked the person next to him, who was local, whether he knew who the short man was. He was told that the man's name was Brian, but other than that he didn't know any more.

"I think I'll rescue him," said Vince, indicating the besieged whisky drinker.

"You're such a Samaritan," responded Dennis, "why don't you mind your own business and enjoy your pint?"

"This could be fun," replied Vince and toddled off towards the end of the bar.

Before he could make any progress the beleaguered man rose from his stool and made his way to the toilet. Vince followed at a discreet distance.

"Having trouble?" asked Vince, as he stood next to the man, both facing the newly installed bucket arrangement.

"Excuse me, with what?" said the man, jumping to the wrong conclusion.

"I'm sorry; I meant your new friend at the bar. I couldn't help noticing that he seemed to be annoying you.  He seems a bit full of himself," said Vince.

"Well, yes, he is a bit bumptious.  He just appeared and introduced himself and now I can't get rid of him. It's not a problem, my wife will be down soon and we'll be off to dinner."

"He seemed to be saying something important," persisted Vince, as he finished his business and turned to the washbasin to wash his hands.

"Yes, he's a developer and he was saying that he never pays tax. He ought to be more careful; you never know who can hear you," offered the man, now also washing his hands.

"How right you are," concluded Vince and held the door open for the other man to exit.

Dennis watched as the boastful developer waited for the middle aged man to return. Fortunately for the latter his wife had by then appeared and he was able to make his excuses and disappear to the restaurant for dinner.

Vince sat back on his seat and nudged him. "Now I know a bit more," he confided. "This could be interesting. I think we need to talk to our short friend. Wait there." He got up again and approached the bar.

"Excuse me, but I couldn't help hearing a little bit of your conversation with your friend who has just left.  Please don't think I'm rude, but I'd like to have a chat with you," he said. "Oh, I'm sorry, how rude of me. My name's Vince," he said, holding out his hand. "Perhaps you'd let me buy you a drink. You're almost empty."

With a fresh pint in his hand Vince invited him to take a seat with them.

"I'm sorry about earlier," began Dennis, "but you know how it is; every man for himself when a seat becomes free.  My name's Dennis.""

"I'm Brian," replied their new friend.

"You were saying over there that you're a developer and never pay tax," Vince began.

Brian became suddenly wary. "You're not from The Revenue, are you?" he asked, "it was only bar talk."

"Don't worry," laughed Dennis. "there's nothing to worry about from us. What you do or don't do is none of our business."

"Thank God," Brian exhaled, "for a moment I thought I was in trouble."

The three men sat chatting for some time and more drinks were consumed. Brian, however, failed to notice that he was drinking twice the amount and at a faster pace than his new friends. The noise in the bar grew louder as the evening wore on and Brian did likewise. During the course of their carefully engineered conversation he had told Dennis and Vince virtually his entire life story and they knew almost everything about him.  They had divulged nothing about themselves, but Brian was too busy boasting to notice.

The need to relieve himself overcame Brian fairly frequently and Dennis and Vince took the opportunities to draw up their plan.  It evolved over the course of the evening until it had been refined into something definite. They knew they would have to make their pitch carefully, but they were consummate salesmen and Brian was sucked into their scheme with ease.  By ten o'clock a firm arrangement had been made and Brian left.

His departure was noticed by several people in the bar, as well as by the landlord.  Dennis and Vince remained seated and surveyed their surroundings. They sipped the remainder of their drinks and discussed the heating installation they were due to begin the next morning. They became part of the scenery once again.

The organiser of The Golden Horseshoe Challenge remained in her seat all evening.  She and her companions enjoyed a substantial bar meal and several bottles of wine.  Her legs remained firmly clamped around the bag on the floor and she didn't seem to loosen her grip at all. Vince thought she must be a woman of remarkable capacity and fortitude because she hadn't felt the need to powder her nose for the best part of three hours. When the group eventually broke up the woman left the bar alone, clutching the bag tightly and she and the rest of her party went their separate ways. She said her farewells to several people and the landlord. She was obviously well known and liked.  Dennis noticed that nobody followed her out and thought that she was taking an enormous risk.

-14-

Mary Trent made her entrance. She had spent the last hour pottering around the Honeymoon Suite, basking in the glow of the afternoon's activity and slowly preparing for the evening meal. She chose her clothes with care, and her make-up was applied with practiced expertise. She opted for a delicate gold necklace and the finishing touch was an expensive gold watch. By the time she was ready she knew she looked good; understated but very attractive. She was a trim figure and she turned heads, but was unaware of her power. She therefore didn't notice Dennis and Vince follow her every move appreciatively. David Trent, her husband, was always aware of men looking at her and was proud. He felt undeserving of such a catch, but was comfortable in the knowledge that they were a devoted couple.

As was her normal custom, she declined a drink at the bar when David offered and as he ushered her before him on the way to their table in the restaurant, he looked over his shoulder at the pair from Manchester and smiled, letting them know he had read their thoughts.

They were greeted by the waitress who had earlier hugged David in warm greeting, and she now welcomed Mary with equal feeling. Their table was immaculately set, with crisp white linen and gleaming silver cutlery and the wine, having breathed for an hour, now in optimum condition.  A bottle of fresh ice cold water had also been place on the table. They sat and the waitress passed them their menus, before discreetly withdrawing to allow them time to settle and read. As usual, they were not disappointed with what was before them.

### *Starters*

Crayfish, Oak Smoked Salmon and Asparagus Salad, on a bed of young Salad leaves with zesty lemon dressing (G)

Homemade Smooth Chicken Liver Pate, with Chef's own Pear, Port and Red Onion Chutney served with hot, crisp toast (G)

Mature Cheddar Cheese Souffle', on a Salad of Baby Leaves and Celery, finished with a savoury Beetroot and Braeburn Apple Coulis (V)

Crab Torte, with a creamy fresh Chive and Tarragon Mayonnaise

Roasted Fig, Prosciutto Ham & Smoked Duck Breast Salad, finished with crisp Croutons and Orange Vinaigrette (G)

Honey Roasted Peach, on a bed of Baby Leaves with toasted Sesame Seeds, finished with a refreshing Summer Berry Dressing (G) (V)

Chef's Homemade Soup of the Day, topped with Crispy Croutons

OR

Sorbet

## *Main Courses*

Fillet of Salmon Pan Fried with Leek and Caper, finished with a splash of White Wine and served with classic Hollandaise. Accompanied by Mange Tout and Julienne Carrots (G)

Grilled Lamb Cutlets with Redcurrant, Port and Rosemary Glaze, served with Apple and Onion infuse Spring Greens (G)

Sea Bass Fillet marinated with Chilli, Lime, Coriander and Ginger. Baked with Pepper, Courgette and Shallot (G)

Breast of Chicken wrapped in Smoked Streaky Bacon, oven baked and served with caramelized Red Onion with a touch of Sage. Completed with Roasted Courgette and Red Pepper (G)

Thatcher's Cider Battered Cod with minted Garden Pea Puree, served with Mange Tout and Julienned Carrots

Roasted Breast of Duck with a Sweet and Sour Plum Sauce, sided with Apple and Onion Spring Greens

Crisp Filo Pastry Nest filled with a Mix of Mediterranean influenced, griddled Vegetables and Creamy Mozzarella (V)

Carvery of the Day with Roast Potatoes and all the Trimmings.

All Main Courses are served with a Choice of Potatoes –

Parsley Butters New Potatoes

Fondant Potato

Or French Fries

(G) indicates Gluten Free (V) suitable for Vegetarians.

### *Grills*

STEAKS –

12oz Rib eye Steak £3.50 Supplement

8oz English Sirloin Steak

(All weights uncooked)

Cooked to your liking and served with Tomatoes and Mushrooms

Choose from Garlic Sauce            Peppered Sauce

Diane Sauce

*Sweets of the Day*

Choose from our selection of Sweets found in the Dessert Menu

All sweets come with a choice of topping-

Pouring Cream    Clotted Cream                Ice Cream

    Custard

Cheese Board

Choose from our extensive selection of local quality cheeses

All cheese comes with a selection of biscuits.

Please ask about our selection of Port.

Coffee with Mints.

"I was hoping the venison would be on," ventured David.

"I'm told it will appear tomorrow," said a voice at his shoulder.

Linda, the owner's wife had spirited herself to their table. "It's

lovely to see you again, Mrs Trent," she said warmly.

"And you. It's good to be here," replied Mary.

"What have you got planned this time?" enquired Linda.

"Oh, we thought we might take a look at this Golden Horseshoe

for the first couple of days," David said.

"Good idea," Linda responded. "It's the fiftieth this year and there is more taking part than ever before.  It should be quite a spectacle."

Where's the best place to see it from?" asked Mary.

"You can find one place and stay put to watch them all come through, although that can be a little tedious, but I think the best thing is to follow it around, if you can.  You have to keep your wits about you, because they go all over the place. You'll see more of the Moor if you do that.  Perhaps even see places you've never seen before. I would latch onto the support vehicles and go wherever they go, if you don't mind narrow lanes. Also, the locals help by dashing about on their Quad Bikes, so you could try to follow them  Oh, I forgot, most of them have been stolen recently, so I doubt you'll see that many. The police have been out and about a lot more lately, obviously looking at the vehicles being used for the Golden Horseshoe.  These good people on the tables either side of you are taking part, so perhaps it would be a good idea to chat with them," Linda explained.

"Thank you," said David, "that's really helpful."

"Enjoy your evening," said Linda and departed as unobtrusively as she had appeared.

"I love it here," said Mary, looking into her husband's eyes, at the same time as rubbing his foot with her own under the table.

"So do I. Don't," he pleaded, colouring slightly, "let's at least have dinner first. "

The restaurant was filling quickly, so they ordered without delay and settled to take in their surroundings.

The table to Mary's right had five occupants, who were Kevin and Karen Wilson and their support team of three. At the table to her left sat Tamsyn Carter and her daughter Katie. Everybody relaxed noticeably as the evening wore on as the fine food, good wine and warm ambience worked their magic.

David introduced himself and his wife to Tamsyn and Katie. Tamsyn had earlier delivered an oral report on her previous year's experience at the meeting for entrants. Their subsequent conversation revealed that they were entering for the second time. Tamsyn was the rider and Katie the support, who would provide water, food, clothes, tack and anything else from the back of their Land Rover. At the end of the meal, a map was produced which showed their route.  David knew roughly where they would be going and tried to work out whether to follow these two for the day.

"I tried to get my husband to come along," said Tamsyn, "but he hates horses."

"Oh, that's a pity," said Mary.

"Yes," continued Tamsyn. "I think he was put off a few years ago when my horse kicked him on the inside of his thigh. Quite high up, actually."

Her daughter, Katie, grinned. "It could have been much worse. At least he managed to turn his leg so that he protected his main assets!"

"We shouldn't laugh," said Tamsyn, smiling broadly. "He's still got the imprint. Gets pain in that area as well. Why do we always laugh when somebody else gets hurt?"

"It's human nature," ventured Katie, failing to hold herself together, as her shoulders shook up and down.

"Well, at least he'll have a few days peace while we're here, and he can eat what he wants," concluded Tamsyn. "There's plenty in the freezer but I bet he's had a takeaway tonight."

Karen Wilson listened intently as the meal progressed, trying to garner any snippets of detail which might help her on her first Golden Horseshoe. Eventually, Kevin's story was told and the entire gathering was at a loss as to how to react. Silence fell and eyes were averted.

"For heaven's sake," said Kevin, "You don't need to avoid it. I've decided to look life in the eye and stare it down. I don't worry about a thing anymore. I wish I'd discovered this approach long ago; I might have done more with my life. We've accepted it all, that's why we're here. Karen has always wanted to do something like this, so we just decided to go for it. If there's one thing I've learned, it's that life is too short to make excuses. How many times do we think we can't do something because there's no time, or opportunity or we let other things get in the way? No! If you want to do something, just get on with it. Don't die wondering."

Having finished his little lecture he sipped his wine and returned to his meal.

"Here ends the lesson," he added, looking at his audience squarely, unflinching and smiling broadly. Karen and the rest of their table laughed with him.

There was also a table, set for two, which was the only unoccupied table in the entire restaurant. It was booked for Dennis and Vince, but events had proved so interesting in the bar, and had gone on for so long, that they decided to eat there.

Finally, there was a table set for eight.  This was a party of tourists from America, who had flown in the previous day, stayed overnight near Heathrow Airport and then travelled by coach to Exmoor. The five women and three men had never met before their trip and each was single and over the age of fifty. As each overcame the effects of jetlag at different rates, the group became increasingly noisy during the evening. Their waiter, named Jake, was assigned to their table alone. Originally from Cornwall, a county further to the west of England, he was a patient, quietly spoken man who was not easily rattled. The three day stay of his particular guests, however, tested even his patience to its breaking point. He found it difficult to maintain his calm exterior as they made even the simple task of ordering a meal as difficult and complicated as possible.  He went around the table, beginning with the women as courtesy demands, noting down the orders for Starters. He then started to take the Main Course orders, but hadn't got past the second woman before one of the men decided to change his Starter choice.  Then another did the same. Others followed suit until he got to the point where he had to start all over again. This problem repeated itself during the process of ordering the Main Course and he had to begin that again as well.

Eventually, after what to him seemed a lifetime, he had it all written down.

"Let's just confirm all this," he said, trying and only just succeeding to keep the acid out of his voice. He then went round the table reading each person's order for Starter and Main. Satisfied that he had at last got an accurate reflection of their wishes, and having ensured each was assigned to the appropriate room's account, he told them he would return immediately after placing the order in the kitchen and left them wine lists.

He rolled his eyes at the chef, who was reading the order, and took a deep breath before turning round for more of the battle. When he arrived at the table, notepad in hand, there was a fierce argument raging about how the bill was to be divided.  Some wanted each room to be dealt with separately, some wanted the bill to be divided equally between the eight people, whilst the others were pushing to have the drinks divided equally with the food was assigned to their rooms. Jake stood patiently as the noise grew and the argument increased in intensity.  Others in the restaurant were ceasing their own conversations as they listened with either amusement or annoyance.

"So," he said, in an attempt to move proceedings along, "what would you like to drink?"

All eight answered in unison and he hadn't got a chance. He stood at the head of the table, pen poised over his pad and waited for the commotion to die down. It proved to be an exercise in futility. Some wanted only a soft drink, some wanted wine, either shared or alone, and one or two wanted to try the local ale.

"Let's go round the table," Jake suggested. "Madam, what would you like?"

"I'd like to try some of your local, what is it called, best bitter?" said a slightly built demure figure who occupied pride of place at the head of the table. This was a fact that clearly irked some of the men, who shot glances that would melt steel in her direction.

"Certainly," responded Jake, who had decided to go with the flow and enjoy the unfolding debacle. "Would that be half a pint or a pint?"

"Oh, make it a pint," she replied, "what the hell, I'm only here once."

"May I take your room number, please?" he asked.

She managed to give the number just as the whole argument kicked off again. To his credit, Jake, the patient Cornishman, moved quietly to the next woman and stayed in position with his pen poised. He bent so that he could speak in her ear.  She responded by ordering her drink and giving the room number.  As this tactic appeared to work, he repeated it for the final woman. The three women now had no need to be part of the shouting match, so sat quietly waiting and watching, but the men had not noticed the process and continued their heated debate. Jake selected one of the men and tried with him.

"Don't you invade my personal space," the man said loudly, before continuing his contribution.

"I'm sorry sir," said Jake.

He took a pace back from the melee and decided that it would be best if he dealt with the drinks for the women to give the men time to settle down.  He stood at the bar as the drinks were prepared and placed on a tray.  He took another deep breath and approached the table of eight.  He couldn't help noticing that the entire restaurant was absolutely silent.  Not a sound could be heard. There was no scraping of plates, no clinking of glasses, no whispered tones; just nothing. Jake looked round the room and was aware that he was the centre of attention.  Not knowing what had occurred, he was somewhat nervous, but covered it well.  He gave the women their drinks and waited for the men to place their orders.  He was dumbfounded as they gave their orders in turn, quietly, calmly and politely without any further fuss. He did, however, spot that the loudest and most difficult of the men was now the most sheepish and was stealing furtive glances at the table which had been empty, but was now occupied by a man and a woman, sitting opposite each other.  There were no other waiters to be seen, so he went to the table to take their order.

"I know we're a little late," said the man, "but I hope not too late. Please fit us in as and when you can; we're lucky to have got a table at all.  We'll be happy to sit here for a while."

"Thank you sir, as you can see, we're quite busy this evening, but I'll be back to take your order shortly," said Jake.

When he returned the restaurant had returned to a relaxed normality. There was no longer tension in the air and all seemed well.  He gave the men their drinks and began to take the order from the two newcomers. He was perplexed.

"What's...?"

"There's no problem," the man interrupted, "nothing to worry about.  When my wife and I came in there appeared to be a hiatus of some sort, centred round that large table over there. One man in particular seemed especially agitated and I asked him to settle down. Peter, the owner came in, after order had been restored and I told him you had managed the situation admirably. I said you should be commended, so I hope he has a word with you."

Jake didn't know what to say. He thanked the stranger and took the drinks order. The man told him to make sure he had one himself, as he undoubtedly deserved it.

"Thank you," said Jake, "I really don't know what's happened here, but I am grateful. What room number is it, sir?"

"Oh, we're not staying here, "replied the man. "We're new to the village and thought we'd try the inn tonight. I didn't think it would be so busy. We're lucky to get in. If its popularity is anything to go by, we'll be eating here a lot."

"Well welcome to you both. I hope you'll be happy here. It's nice and quiet and the folks are really very nice. Tonight isn't typical. My name's Jake," he went on, holding out his hand. He was struck by the strength of the handshake he received and the assured resolve in the man's eyes.

"Thank you. Pleased to meet you. I'm Ray Quinn and this is my wife, Nancy.

## GOLDEN ROBBERY

-15-

The young policeman walked past the Exmoor White Horse Inn, through the misty May air, wondering when the promised downpour would arrive. It was the evening before the Golden Horseshoe Challenge and he knew that there was a very valuable piece of gold at the inn.  The formidable organiser had insisted on keeping it under her own guard, despite many warnings from her high up friends at Taunton police station. She had only informed the police about the item because the insurance company had been insistent. PC Tony Parker had been assigned to keep a watchful, discreet eye on proceedings, without her knowledge or permission.  In fact she would have been affronted if she knew.  It was dark and he had been waiting most of the evening. He was actually dealing with two matters, because apart from maintaining vigil over the actual Golden Horseshoe, he was also in situ to react to any developments on the Quad Bike front.

He crossed the bridge that spanned the River Exe in front of the inn, half listening to the static from his radio, pinned to the front of his uniform. He looked at his watch. He was in a bad mood because he'd spent most of the first part of his shift doing an unpleasant body search for hidden drugs, completing an arrest report and then making sure the idiot, who had initially been pulled over for suspected drunk driving, was safely ensconced for the night in a cell. He had only just got to his position in time to see the local property developer leave the inn, obviously somewhat worse for wear.  He sincerely hoped he was not going to climb into a car and drive away, because he would have been forced to catch up and do the necessary.

The inn was obviously extremely busy, he noted. The car park was full and there was an excited buzz emanating from the entrances and some half closed windows. He wished he was inside sampling his favourite tipple and rounding off the evening with a malt whisky from the well stocked bar.

Tony sidled towards a window, trying to judge what was happening. He held an ambition to become a plain clothes officer and always tried to carry himself as he imagined he would without uniform. He was in his early twenties and it was not easy to make the change as competition was fierce. He had long ago decided that if he was going to make the switch he needed to show the powers that be that he was better than the rest. He was, therefore diligent and thorough. The locals liked him as well, because they knew he was straight and could be relied upon.

Reluctantly he moved away from the window to continue his patrol through the village and walked straight into a robbery. Twenty feet away a man in a hooded mask, with cut outs for his eyes, was pointing something at a female figure.

"No," the woman cried, "don't take it. You can't!"

Tony made no move except to speak softly into his mike. He gave his call sign and location and requested immediate backup. The victim and her assailant heard him say that the man was armed.  The mugger's eyes went wide with fear as the policeman reached down and found his taser. Tony stood gripping the weapon with both hands, standing fore-square to his quarry, his legs braced.

"Put your hands in the air.  Let her go! NOW!" He shouted. "Do it now! Taser,Taser Taser. Do as I say or I WILL use it."

He knew it was not exactly a textbook warning, but he wasn't used to this sort of thing happening in the quiet Exmoor village. The man was panicked. He froze for a moment, and then swung the woman in front of him, using her as a shield. The woman continued to hold her bag desperately.

"Please! Don't take it," she pleaded.

Tony's hands were rock solid on the taser and he remained fixed in position. He caught himself thinking that if this were happening in America he would be holding a Glock and considering deadly force. He wondered what passed through the minds of his colleagues over there when faced with the possibility of killing somebody. He shook his head to clear his mind.  He had no clear target. It was too risky. The assailant had blended into the darkness of the night, despite the meagre street lighting.

"'Don't move," the man said his voice cracking. "I'll kill her."

Tony stood upright and lifted his left hand, palm outward.

"Ok, Ok. Look, nobody's been hurt," he said, "we can work this out. You don't need to make it worse."

"Give it to me," the man snapped at the woman.

"No! No!" The woman turned and swung her fist at the man's head.

"Don't!" Tony cried, certain he would hear the pop of a pistol shot and see the woman fall. He knew he would then have a target, but prayed it wouldn't happen that way. He has used his taser on one previous occasion and the result had not been pleasant.

The man did not shoot, however.  At that moment several people had emerged from the inn and begun to walk in their direction. They saw what was happening and scattered in panic. Some even got themselves between the young police officer and the mugger. The man pulled the bag from the woman's grip, turned and fled. Tony managed to get a sight on his back and started to apply pressure to the trigger, but the man was out of range too quickly. He stopped and lowered the weapon. Gathering himself, he sighed and sprinted after the man, but he had vanished. A moment later Tony heard a car engine start and a grey car skidded away into the distance.  He hadn't even had time to see the number plate or make. He called an update into his radio and ran to the woman who had been robbed. He helped her to her feet.

"Are you alright?" he asked.

"No, I'm not all right,'" the woman spat out, holding her chest. She was bent in agony and her face was bright red, with sweat running down her forehead.

"Have you been shot?" He asked, beginning to panic.

She narrowed her eyes in fury as she straightened up. "No, it's worse. That bag contained the Golden Horseshoe. It's worth more than you can earn in a year," she said, turning her piercing eyes on Tony. "Why the hell didn't you shoot him? Why?"

Ancient Exmoor, with Dunkery Beacon at its highest point, was witnessing another unfolding drama.  There had been many over the centuries, but there was no way of knowing how far reaching it would become.  The urgent screaming of the speeding police car sirens could be heard across the moor, seeming to echo through the night like wailing banshees.

The ambulance was the first emergency service to arrive, followed closely by PC Tony Parker's duty Sergeant and two detectives from the station. Not long afterwards, because word had got out that the Golden Horseshoe had been stolen and the organiser assaulted in the process, four higher ranking detectives from Taunton appeared. Tony realised the woman must have friends in high places and was wary about what could happen next. It also didn't take long for the parasites of the media to arrive. There were more than he'd ever seen in his young life, and they included local television stations as well as the written media. The omens were not good for young Tony.

The woman, who was still immaculate apart from a slight tear in her coat, stood with her arms crossed, anger etched into her face.

She seemed to be having trouble breathing but waved off the medics as if swatting irritating flies. She said to the Sergeant, "this is unacceptable; completely."

The object of her anger, grey haired and resembling a military man, was trying to calm her down.

"Mrs Huntley-Smythe; Miriam, I'm sorry for your loss."

PC Parker noticed that the woman had been addressed by her first name and his heart sunk.

"Loss? Loss?" she repeated for emphasis, "you make it sound as if my credit card has been stolen."

"But there was nothing more PC Parker could do," he continued.

"That man was going to kill me, and he let him get away," she shouted, pointing at Tony. "He let him get away with the prize. There's nothing like it in the world. It's irreplaceable."

Tony thought that couldn't be exactly true, even though he knew it had to be found, or replaced, in less than the next two days.

My colleague did everything by the book," the Sergeant continued, not much interested in the uniqueness of the stolen item.

"Well, the book ought to be changed," the angry woman snapped, not in the least placated.

"I didn't have a clear target," Tony said, angry that he felt the need to defend himself to a civilian. "You can't just go shooting people in the back."

"He was a criminal," Mrs Huntley-Smythe said, "and, my God, it wasn't as if ... I mean, he was black."

Everybody who had heard turned towards her. The Sergeant's face grew still and cold as he heard her words. He glanced at the senior detective, a round man in his forties, who rolled his eyes.

"'I'm sorry," she said hurriedly, trying to make amends, "I meant he had a black hood. I didn't mean anything else. it's just that it was terrifying having someone push a gun into your ribs."

"Hey," a reporter shouted from the crowd, which by now had noticeably grown in size, "how about a statement?"

Tony was about to say something but the detective said, 'no statements at this time. We'll issue a press briefing in about an hour."

Another detective walked up to Tony. "What can you tell us about the assailant?"

Another detective walked up to Mrs Huntley-Smythe. "What can you tell us about the assailant?"

The lady thought for a moment. "Well, I think he was quite short and strong. He wasn't thin. I thought he was black, but that must have been the mask. Thinking about it now, the skin round his eyes was not black."

"Did he have trainers or shoes?"

"I don't know," she replied.

"What about a watch?"

"I can't think. Slow down, please." There was silence for a few moments before she said, "I think it might have been an expensive watch. I didn't see much because he had gloves on."

"Anything else you can remember? Hair colour, his smell? Had he been drinking?"

The redoubtable Miriam Huntley-Smythe was flustered now, reeling not only from the actual attack but also from the barrage of questions which seemed almost as bad. She took her time and drew a large intake of breath to reg

ain her composure.

"I told you, he wore a mask, so I didn't see the colour of his hair, but the hairs on his wrist by his watch were fair, perhaps ginger.

He had alcohol on his breath, but apart from that I can't remember smelling anything."

"Well I think that will be all for now, Miriam. I'll get a colleague to accompany you home and take a look round, just to be sure," said the officer. "I'll be in touch."

"Thank you," she replied. "Wait, I do remember something. He had dust or powder on his gloves."

"What colour?"

"White, I think. At least that was the colour under the light and the moon."

"Thank you. That's very helpful. We'll do everything we can. Goodnight." The detective was terse, but his mind was racing and leaping to conclusions. He called PC Tony Walker to his side. "If he had been drinking there's a good chance he was over there," he pointed at the White Horse Inn. "Tell me. Honestly. We supported you tonight, but could you have tasered him? Did you have a chance?"

"No," Tony said. "When he was facing me I didn't have a clear target and the backdrop wasn't clean. After that all I had was his back, and he disappeared quickly. I had to stop to make sure Mrs Huntley-Smythe was ok first."

"That's fine. I had to check. We'll deal with the fallout, and believe me, there will be a lot. That woman has friends in high places."

Tony had already surmised as much and knew his ambition to become a plain clothes officer could be in jeopardy. He looked at his watch. It was nearly midnight.

"Your shift's over. Write your report and get home," said his Sergeant.

"What about the Quad Bike surveillance?" he asked.

"That will still be there tomorrow, and I've got enough cover on that."

Tony held up a hand. "Can I ask a favour?"

"What?"

"It's about my application for plain clothes."

Tony knew it was sitting in an in-tray along with dozens of others. The wily old Sergeant caught on and grinned.

"You want to help with the case?" he asked.

"No I want all of it," replied Tony.

"Impossible," said the Sergeant, "but as you're so keen, I'll give you some time on it. Half a shift and no overtime and you work with the detectives." He looked into PC Walker's eyes. "You're not going to work with the detectives, are you?"

"No," replied Tony.

The Sergeant debated. "I'll take a chance, but you have to keep me informed. Oh, and you need to get the mugger and the stolen horseshoe. Not much to ask, is it?" he smiled at his enthusiastic young PC. "Also, you don't talk to the media at all. Let somebody else do that. This has all the hallmarks of something that goes pear shaped, and they'll be looking for somebody to crucify, so be careful"

"I understand; and thanks," said Tony.

"Well, get going; the clock's ticking," said the Sergeant. He smiled as his young PC walked away, pleased with himself for giving youth and enthusiasm its opportunity to shine. He wished he had been given the same leeway at the start of his career, but there had been nobody above him with the courage and foresight.

Tony called his wife from the station and told her not to wait up as he was on a special case.

"It's not dangerous, is it?" she said. She was pregnant with their first child and feeling vulnerable.

"No. There's nothing to worry about. They want me to follow something up."

"That's great, well done."

"Get some sleep," he said. "Look after the bump. I love you both."

"We love you too," she replied and put the phone down.

He changed into street clothes and drove away from the station in his own car, as all the unmarked ones were already out and about. The jeans and trainers were only for comfort, since there was no way he would not be noticed where he was going. He was heading for the seediest back street pub in the town and he would stand out like a sore thumb. But that didn't matter; he wasn't there to fool anybody. He'd worked the streets long enough to know there was only one way to get information out of people who weren't otherwise inclined to give it to you: buying and selling. Of course, he didn't have any grass money, being just a PC, normally in uniform, but he thought he had some negotiable tender to shop with.

"Hello Sam,' he called, walking up to the bar.

"Tony. What are you doing here?" the white-haired old barman asked in a raspy voice. "Looking for a game?"

"No, I'm looking for an idiot," said Tony.

"There's plenty of them round here," replied Sam, the barman. "What's he done?"

"Mugged a woman at gunpoint," said Tony, "and it's personal. He got away from me and he's gone to ground."

"That sounds serious," said the barman.

"It will be when I catch him," promised Tony. "How's your brother, by the way?"

"How do you think?" the barman sneered at Tony."How would you like to spend four years inside?"

"I wouldn't like it one bit," affirmed Tony, "but I also wouldn't like being the old woman he beat up for the price of a fix."

"Well, he didn't kill her, did he?" said the barman, becoming angry, mainly because he knew Tony had a point.

"No, but she's still in a home and won't come out again, so don't expect sympathy from me," replied Tony, equally annoyed now. "But let's move on shall we? Do you think he'd like to get out early, maybe do half the sentence?"

Sam poured a beer for Tony. He drank half of it.

"I don't know," Sam said. "I bet he'd like to be looking at one year instead of four."

Tony thought for a minute. "How does eighteen months sound?"

"You're just an ordinary PC. You can't do that, can you?"

Tony decided that he'd have his Sergeant's support. He also thought about the other, more senior officers, who had come rushing to the mugging earlier. The deciding factor for him was the way they had referred to the victim as Miriam. He reasoned that gave him some leverage.

"Yes, I can do it," he said.

"'But listen, I'm no grass," Sam was quick to point out. "I have to be careful round here. I could get badly hurt."

"'I saw him in action. Don't worry. He's a loner, there's no gang, no backup or bully boys," said Tony, crossing his fingers and hoping. "He also picked on the wrong victim and will go inside. It won't be a rap on the knuckles for him."

"Well, have you got a name?" asked the barman.

"No name," replied Tony.

Well, what does he look like?" Sam asked.

"I'm sorry I can't look through masks," said Tony.

"Oh," was all Sam could think of.

"He's short, thick set and strong.  He has fair or ginger hair and wears a fake expensive watch," Tony summarised the description.

"How do you know it's fake?" asked Sam.

"Because he'd be an idiot to wear an expensive one on a job, wouldn't he?" offered Tony. "It might get broken or recognised. Oh, and he plays snooker."

"How do you know that?" Sam was intrigued.

Tony knew because, whatever his detective colleagues may be thinking, whatever lines of enquiry they were chasing, no drug dealer or user would be so careless with cocaine or heroin, that he'd he would leave a dusting of it on his clothes or gloves. If he did he would lick it clean in a second. It had to be the chalk that snooker players use.

"Are you absolutely sure you can swing this for my brother?" asked the barman.

"Yes, I don't make promises I can't keep," replied PC Walker, with everything crossed for luck.

"Eighteen months?" repeated Sam.

"Maximum," promised Tony.

Sam made a quick decision. "There may be somebody," he said. "He's short and stocky. His head shines under the table lights as if it's been polished. He's got ginger hair, that's in a ring round his dome, like a monk or something. Oh, and he does have a fake expensive watch."

"Sounds like it could be the man," said Tony. "How do you know the watch could be fake?"

"Well, he takes it off and puts it on the bar every time he plays. He wouldn't do that with an expensive one, would he?" replied Sam.

"Good point," said PC Tony Walker. "Where can I find him?"

"Why not wait until he comes in again?" suggested the barman. "That way nobody will think I've told you."

"No," replied Tony, "it can't wait.  I need to find him immediately."

"I don't know, this is difficult for me," Sam was wavering.

"Of course, If you can't help me maybe some of my colleagues could visit and check out your records, VAT returns, that sort of thing. Perhaps have a quiet word with one or two of your punters," Tony promised.

"If you put it like that, I don't have a choice, do I?" said Sam

"Not really," Tony said.

Sam hastily scribbled an address onto a scrap of paper and passed it to Tony as if it were a stick of dynamite.

Outside the pub Tony stood debating. If he called for support he knew he would not get the credit for the arrest and recovery.  One of the detectives would claim the glory.  It was just how it worked, he knew.  He had witnessed it for himself. There was a food chain and he was nowhere near the top. He was glad he'd had the foresight to bring his taser with him, but was nevertheless not a little apprehensive.

-16-

Tony stood outside Brian's house.  He could see no other lights anywhere close by and the darkness seemed to envelope him more than usual.  He was on the edge of the moor and it exaggerated his unease. He gradually became aware of music emanating from inside the house. It was a little scratchy; a little squeaky and it reminded him of the sound that a rusty door makes.  It did nothing to calm his nerves, but he listened intently. The violin player worked on some scales, the tone becoming smooth and resonant. Tony leaned against a wall and cocked his head so that he could hear better.  The player broke into some jazzy riffs and it began to sound like there were two people inside the house.

He questioned his decision to do this alone, but told himself that he had no option. It was too late to call for support. He pushed the kitchen door open as quickly and quietly as possible and crept inside. He expected to be confronted, possibly by two men, but the room was occupied by one short, stocky figure with baggy trousers and a violin tucked under his chin.  The bow was gripped in his right hand, hovering above the strings. Tony noticed the watch on his left wrist.

The man's eyes widened in shock at Tony's entrance and he backed away into a corner.

"Stay exactly where you are," ordered Tony. "I'm PC Walker and I need to ask you some questions."

"So why not simply knock on the front door like any normal person?" Brian whispered, his shoulders slumping. "And I hope you've got a warrant."

"Sorry, no warrant," Tony replied, "but I don't think I need one, do you?"

The man let out a sigh. "I recognise you now. You're that copper in the village earlier. Where's your uniform?"

"Is your name Brian?" asked Tony.

"Yes it is," he said. "Brian Devlin."

"Put the violin down and empty your pockets," said Tony. "Carefully, please"

"Oh, I see," said Brian, "there's no need to worry. I'm not armed."

"You had a weapon earlier when you mugged that woman," Tony said.

"No I didn't. She thought it was a gun, but it was only my violin bow. I had it tucked into the sleeve of my coat with the last few inches sticking out. She couldn't see what it was. It served its purpose."

Now that the music had stopped the whole place seemed too quiet to Tony. It was eerie and the air was heavy, as if all sound was being absorbed. He could feel Exmoor closing in around him. The silence was split by static from his radio, and Tony twiddled with it. The mush faded.

"So what happens now?" asked Brian Devlin.

"Well," Tony began, "first you need to give me the item you stole from that woman tonight. You still have it I trust. After that, I'll take you to the station and the whole process begins. It can be long winded I'm afraid, but that's what you get."

"I can't leave the house," Brian stated.

"You don't have a choice," replied Tony. "I'll call for support if necessary."

"There's no need for that," Brian asserted. "It's my mother. She's in her bedroom and she can't be left alone for the night. She needs my care."

"Is there anybody else in the house?" Tony asked.

"No," Brian said.

"I hope you're not lying to me," Tony continued, because that would only make things worse."

"Brian snorted in disgust. "I'm not lying.'

"Empty your pockets. I'm not going to tell you again." Tony ensured he stayed in control.

"Brian did so, slowly. The last pocket gave up the item Tony was looking for, as a cube of chalk settled on the table.

Tony put the handcuffs on his man and felt better.

"Do you live here? He asked.

"Yes," Brian managed. "My mother is here as well."

"So, where's the horseshoe?" Tony demanded.

"In the bottom drawer, down there," Brian indicated a three drawer unit on the other side of the kitchen.

Tony fetched the piece and placed it on the table. It was magnificent and shone brilliantly under the kitchen spotlights. Tony was amused by the thought that it shone more than his prisoner's bald pate.

"'Listen, Devlin, you give me the name of your fence and I'll see what I can do.  I'll tell the CPS you co-operated.," said Tony.

"'I don't have a fence."

"'Bullshit. How were you going to move the gold without a fence?"

"I wasn't going to sell it, I stole it for myself," said Brian Devlin. He smiled and Tony caught the glitter of a gold tooth. I don't need the money," he continued, "I just wanted to see if I could do it."

"You mean, your life is so boring that you need a thrill," said Tony.

"Actually, that just about sums it up. I look after my mother all the time and I don't have time to do anything for myself. I get out to the pub sometimes, but I need more, it's not enough."

"I started to play the violin for her and now I love it myself. It's a kind of therapy. I'd go mad without it," said Brian. "Mother would just fade away if I went down," he finished on a miserable note.

"Let me explain the situation," Tony began. "I witness the mugging of a woman who is well known in this area and has connections in high places. She is naturally upset. No, it's more than that; she is calling for somebody's head. I use my own time to track this thug down and he still has the stolen golden horseshoe. That item is needed as the main prize tomorrow evening. There will be a great many upset and angry people if it's not there. It turns out that this thief, for that is what he is, has an elderly mother who is dependent on him. Oh, and he is a violin nut. This might be my first plain clothes case, but I bet it's not the normal sort of thing my colleagues deal with."

Brian took a breath and was about to contribute, but Tony cut him off.

"Now, let me explain my dilemma," Tony went on. "The straightforward thing to do is to haul your backside down to the station and charge you.  You'll stay in the cells and your mother will be looked after by Social Services. The problem is that this golden thing on the table in front of us wouldn't be available for the prize-giving tomorrow, because it'll be impounded and kept as evidence. Also, it does not deal with the problem of all that money you owe to our lovely tax people. There's income from property, capital gains, not to mention VAT. I'm no expert, but I bet there's more just waiting to be found. Also, some people may think it unfair that the taxpayer has to foot the bill for your mother to be looked after."

Brian Devlin just stood with his mouth agape. This young PC obviously knew all his business and was in his kitchen, large as life, playing with his future and, unforgivably in his eyes, that of his beloved mother. Tony Walker sat down on a kitchen stool and concentrated.  After what seemed like nearly an hour to Devlin, but was actually only a few minutes, he had made up his mind. He handcuffed Brian Devlin to the immovable kitchen table and walked outside into the darkness to radio his Sergeant. When he returned he addressed his prisoner.

"I've explained the situation and my dilemma," he began, "now for the decision. You will listen very carefully. Don't interrupt or I may change my mind."

-17-

At precisely ten o'clock the next morning Tony walked into his police station, carrying the bag containing the Golden Horseshoe in his left hand. He was immediately ushered into a large office and was met by Miriam Huntley-Smythe, his Sergeant and a hand-picked group from the media. Brian Devlin followed in his wake. He waited until the room had fallen silent before handing the bag to his prisoner, who took a deep breath and passed it to Mrs Huntley-Smythe.

'Thank you," was all she managed to say.

Brian held out his hand, but the gesture was studiously and blatantly ignored.

"Why isn't he in handcuffs?" she asked, turning to the Sergeant, who looked at Tony, silently asking the same question.

"Why would I handcuff the man who recovered the horseshoe?" said Tony, shaking his head.

"Why have you got a violin case as well?" asked the Sergeant.

"Ah, well, Mr Devlin here has kindly agreed to play, free of charge, at the prize-giving. Believe me, he's good. I know my music and I've never heard anything like it," said Tony with a butter wouldn't melt smile. "Why don't you demonstrate for us now?" suggested Tony. "I hope you like it, Mrs Huntley-Smythe.

"So do I!" Devlin said with feeling.

"We haven't got time for this," said one detective.

"Just listen, please," replied Tony.

Brian Devlin picked up the violin and played as if his life depended on it. As he warmed to the task the sound became rich and smooth as the room filled with Bach and nobody moved. Brian was playing for his beloved mother way back in his childhood. He finished with 'Love Changes Everything' before letting his arms fall to his side. Everybody was stunned into silence; even hardened police officers were close to tears. There was a prolonged silence.

"Tell us what happened,' a reporter called.

Tony stepped forward and cleared his throat. "I spotted the attack in progress and gave chase. I couldn't catch the assailant, but this man here, Brian Devlin, at great risk to himself, managed to intervene and tackled the mugger. He was able to rescue the horseshoe." Tony was worried that it might sound too rehearsed, which it was, but took comfort from the fact that people are used to the particular way police report things. The public don't believe them if they speak too much like people do normally. There is a degree of officialdom needed. There is a great resemblance between the mugger and Mr Devlin, but that has transpired to be pure coincidence."

The assembled throng shuffled papers and looked at him dubiously.

"I asked Mr Devlin here to join us so that he could explain these developments and to show you how grateful we are for his assistance," Tony went on.

"At first he did not want the publicity, but I insisted he come," added Miriam Huntley-Smythe. "As the victim I also wanted to show my gratitude. I am pleased to announce that Mr Devlin will do us the honour of playing for us at the prize-giving for the competition the night after next. You have all heard his talent. I believe we are lucky to have secured his services. You may not know this, and I am sorry if this causes you embarrassment Mr Devlin, but our new friend here has played at the Royal Albert Hall with the Royal Philharmonic Orchestra. He only returned to live here in order to care for his mother. He had to forego a most promising career. He has been a modest member of the community."

Brian Devlin coughed into his clenched fist and blushed.

"I believe there is a reward for the safe return of the horseshoe," said a reporter.

"Yes there is," she said, "five thousand pounds."

Tony Walker frowned and whispered something into the woman's ear.

"Of course," she said quickly, "my mistake. It's actually ten thousand pounds."

There was a general murmur and people began to discuss this revelation. The Sergeant took the opportunity to crook his finger toward Tony, and they huddled in a corner.

"What the hell is going on?" he demanded.

"It's just as you've heard," answered Tony, his face an angelic picture of innocence.

"This isn't going to do your chances of plain clothes any good, you know," said the Sergeant.

"I know," said Tony, "but look at it this way. Mr Devlin is selling his rental properties to pay for his mother's care home fees. She's going to get the best money can buy. That also means that he won't be getting income from them and not declaring it and he'll have to repay whatever the taxman thinks he owes as well. In addition, he'll still have to pay the Capital Gains Tax. Oh, I almost forgot; he won't be getting the reward money. That was put up by the insurance company, and Mr Devlin has kindly offered to donate it charity."

"Did he have a choice in any of this?" asked the Sergeant, who by now was almost lost for words.

"Not really. He didn't take much persuasion, though. I think he preferred the arrangements to the alternative," answered Tony.

"You know you had no authority for all this, don't you?" the Sergeant continued.

"Of course, I do," replied Tony, "but I think the redoubtable Miriam Huntley-Smythe can persuade those in high places to agree. It's a clean result, I reckon. Don't forget we have an edge on our Mr Devlin from here on in. He can't put a foot wrong and I think he has information about fencing stolen items on a national scale that he'd like to share with us."

The Sergeant knew when to give up and Tony turned to join the assembled throng. His Sergeant excused himself and left, claiming he had a mountain of paperwork to shift. He also told Tony to make sure the entire episode was in writing, on his desk, before he left the building. Tony groaned inwardly. He knew that meant several hours of the sort of grind he hated most. In his view the best place for the majority of paperwork he'd ever experienced was filed in a receptacle labelled 'R'.

Gradually the gathering dispersed and Tony dragged his feet towards a desk and computer keyboard. Several hours later he pressed the 'print' button and waited for his work of fiction to be issued. He then knocked on his Sergeant's door and waved the document at him. In return he was given one sheet of paper confirming his transfer, with immediate effect, to plain clothes.

## THE HONEYMOON SUITE DOOR

### -18-

David and Mary Trent had spent a most agreeable evening in the restaurant. The meal had lived up to its usual high standard, the service had been first class and friendly and they had consumed just enough wine to make them relaxed whilst ensuring the rest of their evening would go equally as well. They spent some time in harmonious conversation with new found friends and decided to follow Tamsyn and her horse Dobbin in the morning as they set out on the Golden Horseshoe Challenge. They were looking forward to experiencing parts of Exmoor they had not yet seen.  Hand in hand and in good humour they climbed the stairs to The Honeymoon Suite.

David had earlier joked that it seemed odd to him that a middle aged man with a heart condition should risk booking The Honeymoon Suite. They were long past honeymoon, after all. Surely it was tempting fate.  He had taken his medication before going for a pre dinner drink at six o'clock and his bedtime pills waited in the room. He slid the key-card down the groove and waited for the electronic click. There was none. He tried again with the same result. He frowned and turned the card round, so that the metal strip faced the other way. Nothing. Once more. Nothing. He turned the card another way but it was to no avail. He looked at his wife.

"Do stop messing about," she said.

"I'm not," he replied. "I can't get it to work."

"Here, let me try," Mary said, gently pushing her husband aside. "It takes a woman to do something technical."

"Be my guest," he said, irked at the hold up. It was ironic that she claimed technical prowess because he had never known anybody with less skill in that direction. It was one of the things for which he loved her. She knew she was no good with that sort of thing and she mocked herself for it on his behalf. Clever woman.

Mary tried several times and had an equal lack of success.

"Stay there," David said, "I'll go to Reception."

He descended the stairs with less than good grace. Why is it, he thought to himself, that nothing is easy? They'd had a good evening, he wanted it to continue without delay and he knew his wife felt the same. He found Hayley at the desk. She had been there ever since he and his wife had discovered the inn some years ago, and had become more of a friend than anything else.

"Hello, David," she greeted him. "I saw that you were here again. It's good to see you.  I hope Mary's well."

"She's fine, thank you, Hayley. I've no need to ask about you. You look as lovely as ever." A bit of flattery never did any harm.

Hayley blushed, as she always did.  She couldn't help it. There was something about him, but she couldn't put her finger on it. The voice; the eyes? Both, but there was more than that, she thought. Mary could have told her it was also his hands. They could work wonders, but nobody else would ever have the privilege.

"I have a problem," David interrupted her musing, "we can't seem to get the key-card to work. The door won't open."

"Oh," Hayley said, "That's no good, especially in The Honeymoon Suite! Let me give it a try. I'll bring the master card as well."

Hayley was unable to gain entry either with the specific room card or her master version.

"Peter and Linda have gone to Taunton for dinner with friends. I know the locksmith was here earlier, but I don't think he did any work on your room. I'll phone him."

Hayley talked with the locksmith who told her that he had actually made adjustments to the door of The Honeymoon Suite, but confirmed that it was working perfectly when he left the inn. He said he would call in first thing in the morning, but could not do anything until then. Hayley was not pleased.  She had been left as Duty Manager it was up to her to solve the problem.

"We have a problem, Mr Trent," she admitted. In her experience it was always better to be straightforward with people. "The locksmith can't be here until morning, so I can put you in another room for tonight. I know it won't be like The Honeymoon Suite, but we'll make an adjustment for that."

David and Mary, although obviously disappointed, were more concerned about something else.

"Normally, we would go with the flow.  You're doing what you can and I appreciate it's difficult for you, but I have medication in the room that I have to take tonight.  It's risky for me not to," David said.

"Ah," Hayley was stuck for a moment. "I think I'd better phone Peter."

A few minutes later she emerged from her office and told the stranded couple that Peter and Linda would return as quickly as possible and he would make sure the room could be entered.  In the meantime she suggested they go the bar and offered free drinks for as long as it took.

"That's fine," said David. He realised that the poor woman was doing all she could. Also, he knew Peter would be as good as his word, so there was no point in making any fuss.

"Thank you for being so understanding," Hayley said as she took the couple to the bar and issued instructions to the barman. "The barman knows you drink whisky, and he knows which one. He also knows what you like, Mary, so it's on its way. He will look after you. Don't be afraid to ask for more."

"Don't worry, we won't take advantage," said David with a smile.

Things weren't so bad after all, he thought. The four poster bed was out of reach temporarily, but at least his next favourite activity was sitting there on the table in front of him. He would treat it as after dinner drinks. There was nothing else for it. He hoped Peter took his time.

"They won't be long," said Hayley, "Linda's driving and she's not slow. She gave me a lift once and I still haven't recovered. She frightened the life out of me. She's got a Subaru and it goes like a rocket. It's no wonder Peter's going grey.

Exactly forty five minutes, two whiskies and two red wines later, they walked into the bar. Peter had obviously suffered an experience that would stay with him for a long time and was grateful to have arrived in one piece.  Linda, however, was all smiles. She had thoroughly enjoyed her dash through the dark lanes and the adrenalin coursing through her veins put her in good humour.

"One door expert, delivered personally," she laughed. "Perhaps he may need one of those," she went on, pointing at David's whisky.

"He can speak for himself, you know," Peter found his voice. "I'll have a drink as soon as I've solved this problem.

"In that case I'll stay here with our guests and be sociable," Linda decided and took the drink that the barman had already prepared for her.

"I'm afraid I can't stay after the end of my shift," said the barman, "I've got something arranged."

"That's no problem." Linda said, "I'll do the necessary."

"I'd be quite happee to stay for as long as necessaree," called a new voice, as one of the waiters entered the bar area, his work having been completed in the restaurant. I only have a short walk 'ome." he added brightly, spotting an opportunity to have a drink or two and further his career. The man was of French origin and in his thirties. He had worked at The Exmoor White Horse Inn for a few years. He was popular with customers and staff alike as he had an easy going manner. Nothing seemed to worry him and many returning guests (particularly the women, he noted) engaged him in long conversations as they particularly enjoyed his French accent. His favourite topic was football and anything else guests wanted to discuss. He was a clever man and had taken to supporting the same football team as Peter. Whether he thought this would ensure continued employment or not, nobody knew, but the two of them often disappeared up to London on football related activities. He used a Gallic shrug which had become much imitated by colleagues. In his spare time he gave guided walking tours on Exmoor and would often pick up extra income in this way via his contact with guests at the inn.

The four of them sat, talked and drank for over an hour as Peter chiselled away upstairs. He had failed to get any of the key cards to work, so had resorted to old fashioned carpentry. With mallet and chisel in hand he carefully removed the wooden door surround, close to the lock. He tried to be as quiet as possible, but a good volume of noise was impossible to avoid. Progress was slow and somewhat painful as he hit fingers and thumbs, but he resisted the urge to curse and swear.  He was conscious that guests in nearby rooms were inevitably being disturbed, but could think of no way round the problem.  He was surprised and thankful that nobody emerged from a room to investigate or complain.

The reason that nobody complained was that nobody had returned to the rooms closest to The Honeymoon Suite after dinner. Their occupants, the American visitors, had decided, before the saga of the door had begun, to hold an after dinner bonding session in an effort to overcome their earlier misbehaviour in the restaurant.  The three women were finding the local ale very much to their liking and were downing it by the pint at an ever increasing speed, whilst their male counterparts were becoming acquainted with, and increasingly partial to, some of the 150 malt whiskies stocked in a specialist section of the bar.

The French waiter, whose name was Philippe, had followed them to the bar to keep a professional eye on them and was pleased to find David, Mary and Linda there as well, as it meant he could join them whilst carrying out his duty. The final person to arrive and join the late night gathering was Peter and Linda's son,

Ian.  He was a professional fisherman and had represented his country and, indeed, Europe, in competition on many occasions. He helped his parents at the inn whenever he was not away, and also, like Philippe, picked up extra income by taking fishing trips on Exmoor for guests of the inn. It had become a popular activity and many guests booked their stay specifically with fishing in mind.

In common with all fishermen, Ian was not short of a story or two. And so it was that tables were moved, chairs arranged and the Americans, Linda, Philippe, David and Mary settled down to listen.

"You haven't heard this story, Mum," said Ian, looking at Linda. "Let me take you all fishing," he said and spread his arms in a gesture of welcome. He was a king holding court, at least for a short while.

# AN EXMOOR FISHING TALE

## -19-

"My story concerns a small girl named Becky, and her father and mother. The girl is at an age when she is beginning to be aware of the wider world, but is still innocent of its dangers. Her father's hobby is fishing," Ian began. "Oh and don't forget, this is to help pass the time."

"Do you have to go, Daddy? I don't want you to," Becky implored.

"Time to get out of that bed, young lady," said her father, ignoring her plea.

"I don't want you to go out today," she went on.

"And what's my favourite girl worried about?" he asked.

"I don't know; nothing, I just don't want you to go," she repeated.

Jack sat on the edge of his daughter's bed and hugged her. He felt the warmth of her body, surrounded by the peculiar, heart-swelling smell of a child waking. From the kitchen he heard a pan clatter, then another, followed by water running and the refrigerator door slamming. It was Sunday morning. It was early: six-thirty.

She rubbed her eyes. "I was thinking ... what we could do today is we could go to the seaside. You said we could go there soon. And if you have to go fishing, I mean really have to, we could fish in the sea or the rock pools, like we did that time. Remember?"

Jack shivered in mock disgust."'What sorts of fish do you think I'd catch there? Little ones with three eyes and scales that glow in the dark," he joked.

"You don't have to go fishing. We could just walk around and see what we can find," Becky persisted.

He looked out of the window at the dim, grey horizon of the Moor. The whole world seemed asleep, and probably was ...

"Please Daddy? Stay home with us"

"We played all day yesterday,' he pointed out, as if this would convince her that she could do without him today. He was, of course, aware that children's logic and that of adults bore no resemblance to each other. We went up on the Moor and saw some pheasants, and then we went to Dunster to look at the castle."

"But that was yesterday!" she said.

Youngsters' logic, Jack decided, was by far the most compelling.

"And what did you eat at the shop in Dunster?" When logic failed, he was not above diversion.

The eight year old tugged at her nightgown. "Chocolate ice cream,"

"Never" He looked shocked."No"

"You know I did, you were there. Don't be silly," she said with emphasis.

"How big was it?" he teased.

"You know!" she said, laughing now.

"I know nothing, I remember nothing," he said.

"Thisssss big." She held her hands far apart.

Jack said "that's impossible. You would've blown up like a balloon and exploded!" Becky broke into giggles under his tickling fingers.

"Up and at 'em," he announced. "Let's have breakfast together before I go."

"Daddy," she persisted, but Jack had escaped from her room.

He assembled his fishing tackle, stacked it by the door and walked into the kitchen. He kissed his wife, Sue, on the back of the neck and slipped his arms around her as she worked her magic with the eggs in the pan. Pouring orange juice for the three of them, Jack said, "she doesn't want me to go today. She's never complained before."

In the last year he'd taken off a day or two every month to go fishing on the Moor. It was his only relaxation and it gave him peace. He didn't know what he would do without it. His wife placed the cooked breakfast on the table and glanced down the hall where their daughter wandered sleepily into the bathroom and shut the door behind her.

"Becky was watching television the other night," Sue said, "I was finishing some marking and wasn't paying attention.  The next thing I knew she ran out of the room crying. I didn't see the programme, but I looked it up in the Guide. It was some made for TV movie about a father who was kidnapped and held hostage. The kidnapper killed him and then came after his wife and daughter. I think there were some pretty graphic scenes. I talked to her about it but she was pretty upset."

Jack nodded slowly. He'd grown up watching horror films and westerns. In fact he found the cinema a sanctuary from his abusive, temperamental father. As an adult he'd never thought twice about violence in films or on TV, until he became a father himself. Then he immediately began censoring what Becky watched. He didn't mind that she knew death and aggression existed; it was the gratuitous, overtly gruesome carnage that popular shows included that he wanted to keep her from. He was particularly concerned about the violence portrayed in computer games. He wanted to shield her, to protect her, but he knew she, like all growing children, would have to face unpleasant things.

"'She's afraid I'm going to get kidnapped while I'm fishing?"

"She's eight. It's a big bad world out there." Sue said.

It was so difficult with children, he reflected. Teaching them to be cautious of strangers, aware of real threats, but not making them so scared of life they couldn't function. Learning the difference between reality and make believe could be tough for adults, let alone youngsters.

A few minutes later the family was sitting around the table, Jack and Sue flipping through the Sunday Times, reading portions of stories that seemed interesting. Becky, accompanied by her stuffed bear, methodically ate first her bacon, then her eggs and finally a bowl of cereal. She pretended to feed the bear a spoonful of cereal and asked thoughtfully, "why do you like to go fishing, Daddy?"

"It's relaxing."

"Oh." The bits of cereal were in the shape of some cartoon creatures, but Jack didn't recognise them.

"Your father needs some time off. You know how hard he works."

As the creative director of a Bristol advertising agency, Jack regularly clocked up sixty- and seventy-hours per week, and the travelling was also extremely wearing.

"I thought you had a secretary, Daddy. Doesn't she do all your work?"

Her parents laughed together. "No gorgeous, "Sue said, "she helps Daddy with the boring bits, so that he can think and be creative."

"Fishing helps me relax," Jack said, looking up from the sports pages.

"Oh." Becky said, and frowned in concentration as another thought sprang to the front of her mind.

Sue packed his lunch and filled a thermos flask of coffee.

"Daddy?" She was moody again and stared at her spoon before letting it sink into her bowl. "Have you ever been in a fight?"

"The things you think of!" he laughed. She must have a reason for asking, he thought, so decided to answer truthfully.

"Yes, actually, I had a fight when I was at school."

"Did you beat him up?"

"I wouldn't say I beat him up, Becky. He was being a bully and I waited round a corner for him and when he came running past I hit him."

She nodded, swallowed a herd, or school, of shaped cereal objects and set her spoon down again. "Could you beat up somebody now?"

"I don't believe in fighting. Adults don't have to fight. They can talk out their disagreements."

"But what if somebody, like a robber, came after you, could you knock him out?"

"Angel," Jack leaned forward and put his hand on the girl's arm. You know that the things they show on TV, like that movie you saw are all made up. You can't think real life is like that. People are basically good."

"I just wish you weren't going today."

"Why today?"

She looked outside. "The sun isn't shining."

"Ah, but that's the best time to go fishing; The fish can't see me coming. Hey, small person, tell you what, shall I bring you something?"

Her face brightened. "Really?"

"Of course, what would you like?"

"I don't know. Wait, yes, I do. Something for our collection."

"Like last time?"

"You bet, Becky. No problem."

Last year Jack had seen a counsellor. He'd come close to a breakdown, struggling to juggle his roles as overworked executive, husband of a schoolteacher, father and put upon son (his own father, often drunk and always unruly, had been placed in an expensive mental hospital that Jack could barely afford). The therapist had told him to do something purely for himself - a hobby or sport. At first he'd resisted the idea as a pointless frivolity but the doctor firmly warned that the relentless anxiety he felt would kill him within a few years if he didn't do something to help himself relax. After considerable thought Jack had taken up fishing, which would get him away from the city, and then collecting, which he could pursue at home.  Becky, with no interest in the 'yucky' sport of fishing, became his co-conspirator in the collecting department.

Jack would bring home the items and the girl would log them into the computer and mount or display the collectibles. Lately they'd been specializing in watches.

This morning he asked his daughter, "Now, young lady, is it okay for me to go off and catch us dinner?"

'I suppose so," the little girl said, though she wrinkled her nose at the thought of actually eating fish. But Jack could see some relief in her blue eyes. When she'd wandered off to play on the computer Jack helped Sue with the dishes. "She's fine," he said. "We'll just have to be more careful about what she watches. The problem is mixing up make-believe and reality. Hey, what is it?" For his grim-looking wife continued to dry what was already a very dry plate.

"Oh, nothing; it's that I never really thought about you walking off to the wilderness alone before. I mean, you always, think about somebody getting mugged in the city but at least there are people around to help. And the police are just a few minutes away."

Jack hugged her. "This isn't exactly the outback here.  It's Exmoor."

"I know, but I never thought to worry till Becky said something."

He stepped back and shook a stern finger at her. "All right, young lady, no more TV for you either."

She laughed in return and gave him an affectionate pat. "Hurry home; and clean the fish before you get back. Remember that mess last time?"

"Yes, I do," he said, recalling the embarrassment.

"Hey, Jack," she asked, "were you really in a fight at school?"

He glanced toward Jessica's room and whispered, "It lasted about three seconds. I hit when he came round the corner, he looked at me and fell down. That was it. He was a bully and had it coming."

She kissed him and whispered, "come home soon. We'll be waiting for you."

Jack turned off the narrow road onto the Moor. The four wheel drive Range Rover coped with ease as he drove farther into the dense vegetation. Jack decided that he agreed with his daughter: The Moor needed sunlight to be seen at its best. The sky was grey and windy and the leafless trees were black from an early-morning rain. Fallen branches and logs lay scattered like petrified bones.

Jack felt the familiar anxiety twisting in his stomach, recognising the signs of tension and stress: the banes of his life. He breathed slowly, forcing himself to think comforting thoughts of his wife and daughter. Come on, boy, he told himself, I'm here to relax. That's the whole point of it. Relax. He drove another half mile across the deserted Moor. The temperature wasn't cold but the threat of rain, he supposed, had scared off the weekend fishermen. The only vehicle he'd seen since leaving home was a dilapidated farm truck, mud splattered and dented. He drove fifty yards farther on and parked.

The airy smell of the water drew him forward as he walked with his tackle box and rod in one hand and his lunch and thermos in the other. His tackle consisted seven weight lines of varying densities, some leaders of six pounds or so and a net.  He had included black and peacock flies and a few mini lures and hoppers. He had been careful to go for blacks and browns for the colours as most food expected by the fish he sought is dark in colour. He was after Rainbow Trout, Brown Trout and possibly unusual varieties of Blue and Tiger Trout.  He trudged over small, moss covered hummocks and passed a tree with seven huge black ravens sitting on it. They seemed to watch him as he walked beneath their skeletal perch. Then he broke from the trees and looked over the water of Clatworthy Reservoir.  From his vantage point, high at the top of a steep slope, he was struck by its iridescent grey, choppy water, which smoothed closer to the shoreline to an almost linen texture. Like many local fishermen he knew most of its secret bays. He was also aware that it was, in places, almost a scary one hundred feet deep. Some places made him feel sad and although this wasn't one of them, it didn't help his uneasiness either. He closed his eyes and breathed in the clear air. Rather than calming him, though, he felt a surge race through him. It was a fear of some sort, raw, electric and he spun round, certain that he was being watched. He couldn't see a soul, but he was not convinced that he was alone; the woods were too dense, too entangled. Someone could easily have been spying on him from a thousand different nooks.

Relax, he told himself, stretching the word out. Work is behind you.  You're here to get rid of its tensions and stress. He fished energetically for an hour and began to settle. Then he heard the snap of a branch behind him and a painful chill shot down his back. He turned quickly and studied the woodland, but saw nothing. Selecting a different lure, Jack glanced down at the perfectly ordered and cleaned toolbox he used for tackle. He saw his spotless, honed fishing knife. He had a fleeting memory of his father, years ago, pulling off his belt, wrapping the end around his fist and beating the young Jack for leaving one of his tools outside to rust. He had taught Jack to respect his tools. He had beaten it into him to oil the ones that rust, dry the ones that warp and keep knives as sharp as razors. He knew his father's educational method was wrong. He knew he could teach Becky to live without resorting to losing his temper, without beatings, without screaming, without all the traumas he remembered and so deeply resented, but couldn't shake off.

Hr recalled the earlier conversation with Becky about fighting and it made him anxious. Jack avoided confrontation and tended to seek the easy way out of a problem. Perhaps if he had stood up to his father he would not now be so stressed, so anxious about dealing with situations.

He half-heartedly cast a few more times, then hooked the lure into the bail of his reel and began to walk along the shore. He stepped from rock to rock carefully, looking down all the time, mindful of the slippery rocks. He almost tumbled into the cold, black water as he stared at the reflections of the fast clouds. He failed to see the man until he was only ten or twelve feet from him. Jack stopped. He was in his mid forties, dressed in jeans and a checked shirt. He was gaunt and wiry and his face was fox-like, with a few days growth of beard. His right hand held a metal pipe over his head, and his left hand gripped the tail of a large fish as it thrashed and shimmered against a rock. He glanced at Jack and slammed the pipe down on the fish's head, killing it instantly. He threw it into a bucket and picked up his rod and reel.

"Having much luck?" Jack asked.

The man nodded. "A little," the man replied and eyed Jack from head to toe, as if measuring him for a purpose. He then walked to the shoreline and began casting.

Jack felt his anxiety flutter like the ravens' wings. The man's reluctance to converse was odd because fishermen were usually among the friendliest of sportsmen, willing to share information about equipment and technique. It's not difficult to be polite, Jack thought. He'd told Becky that if people behaved the way they should, the decent way, the world would be a different place; no hate, no anger, no boys growing up to become anxious men.

Jack tried again. "What time do you make it?"

The man looked at his watch, but said "about midday," after looking up at the sky.

"That's a nice piece," Jack said. "It looks like it's a compass as well as a watch." Jack nodded at a nearby bench. "Do you mind if I have my lunch here?"

"Whatever," was all the man could muster.

Jack hated that phrase, and the man's rudeness was beginning to grate. He sat down, opened the bag and pulled out his sandwich and apple. His hand touched something else and he found a piece of drawing paper. He looked down at a drawing that Becky had done with the coloured pencils he had given her. It showed a shark, teeth bared, being reeled in by a muscular fisherman. Underneath she had written: 'Fish beware, my Daddy's out there.'

He smiled and his anxiety dissipated as he slowly munched on his sandwich and opened his flask. He was aware of the other man studying him again. "Want a cup of coffee?" he called.

"Can't, it upsets my stomach," replied the man, without even a word of gratitude for the offer. He gathered up his tackle and walked to a tree stump which had been sawn off about three feet from the ground so that it could be used as a table. Its surface was stained deep red. He put his bucket beside it and pulled a fish out. He knew what he was doing as he beheaded it quickly with a sharp knife and slit open the slick stomach, scooping out the entrails with his fingers. He tossed the head and the guts ten feet away into a cluster of waiting ravens and they began to fight noisily over the wet, sticky flesh. The man tossed the cleaned carcass back into the bloody bucket.

Jack looked around and saw that they were completely alone. The only sound was the faint lapping of lake water and the squabbling of the birds. He started to take a bite of his sandwich, but the sight of the crows and their bloody meal put him off. It was then that he noticed a sheet of paper fluttering in the breeze on the ground. It had obviously been blown off a notice board. He was curious and walked over to pick it up. Although the sheet was waterlogged he could still make out the words. The notice was warning and he felt an uneasy twist within him as he read. It offered a reward for information leading to the arrest of a killer who had accounted for four people in the last twelve months. They had all been knifed to death, but robbery was not involved, as only a few personal items were missing in each case. The only information about identification was that the man was thought to be in his mid forties and slim Jack's skin felt hot and he looked up towards the fisherman. He was gone. His tackle was still there, but the man had simply left everything and vanished into the woods. Jack stared at the tackle for a while, until he noticed that the man's knife was gone. The notice fell from his fingers. He studied the dense woods again, completing a full circle. He saw nothing; no sight and no sound. Jack gulped down the last of his coffee, which suddenly tasted bitter, and took a deep breath. His daughter's entreaty for him not to go filled his brain. Calm down, calm down, he forced himself to breathe deeply and slowly. His hands were shaking as he started along the path through the rocks.

He only got a few yards. His boot slid off a smooth rock and he tumbled into a shallow ravine. His tackle box fell open and the contents scattered onto the damp ground. Jack landed on his feet but pitched forward into a rock and rolled onto his back, cradling his leg. He cried out. Moaning loudly, he rocked back and forth. "Oh, it hurts; oh God ."

He heard a shuffle of feet and the scrawny fisherman was looking over the rock at him. His face was flecked with blood from the energetic fish cleaning. Behind him the crows cawed madly.

"My ankle," Jack gasped.

"I can help," he said slowly. "Don't you move." But rather than climbing down the short distance Jack had fallen, the man disappeared behind a tall outcrop of rock.

Jack moaned again and started to call out to the man but he stopped when he realised there was no response. He listened carefully and heard nothing. But a moment later the man's footsteps began to approach, from behind. He had circled around and was walking toward Jack through a narrow alley between two huge rocks. Still clutching his leg with his hands, he felt his heart pounding with the dreaded anxiety. Jack slid around so that he'd be facing the man when he arrived. The footsteps grew closer.

"Hello?" Jack called in a gasp.

No response. The sound of boots on sand became boots on rocks as the dishevelled man approached. He carried a small metal box in his left hand. He paused, standing directly above Jack, looking him over.

"I could have told you those rocks are slippery. There's a safer way round. Let me take a look at that ankle. Don't worry; I used to be a paramedic." He crouched and added," I apologise for earlier, it's just that since the killings round here, I'm wary of everybody."

Jack leapt to his feet, sweeping up his own knife. He stepped behind the astonished fisherman and caught him in a neck lock. He smelled unclean hair, dirty clothes and the piquant scent of fish entrails. He jammed the knife home, and the man's voice wailed in a piercing scream. As he worked the blade slowly up to the shuddering man's breastbone, Jack was pleased to find, as with his other victims, that the anxiety that had been boiling within him vanished immediately. He also noted that playing the injured fisherman was still an effective way to put his victims at ease. He slowly eased the man to the ground, where he lay on his back, quivering. Jack glanced around but the place was still deserted. He bent low and examined the man carefully. No, he wasn't quite dead yet though he soon would be, perhaps before the crows started to work on him. Perhaps not.

Jack climbed back up to the path and had a second cup of coffee. This one he enjoyed immensely; Sue was truly a master with the espresso maker. Then he cleaned the blood from the knife meticulously. Not only because he didn't want any evidence to connect him to the crime but simply because Jack had learned his lesson well; he always oiled, dried and sharpened.

Later that night Jack returned home to find Becky and Sue sitting on the couch in front of the television, sharing a huge bowl of popcorn. He hugged them both hard.

"How's the world's best daughter?"

"We missed you, Daddy. We baked some cakes today. I haven't eaten them all, I saved some for you."

He winked at his wife, who was pleased to find him in such a good mood. She was more pleased still when he told her that all the fish he'd caught were below size and he'd had to throw them back.

"Did you bring me something, Daddy?" Becky asked coyly, tilting her head and letting her long blonde hair hang down over her shoulder.

Jack thought, as he often did that she'd be a heartbreaker someday.

"Of course. Don't I always?" he said.

"Is it something for our collection?" she asked.

"Yes." He dug into his pocket and handed her the present.

"What is it, Daddy?" His heart hummed with contentment to see her take the watch in her hand. "Look, Mommy, it's not just a watch. It's got a compass in it. And it fits on your belt. This is great."

"Do you like it?" he asked.

"I'll make a special box for it," the girl said. "'I'm glad you're home, Daddy."

His daughter hugged him hard, and then Sue called to them from the dining room, saying that dinner was ready and could they please come and sit down.

~~~~~~~~~~~~~~~~~~~~~~~~~~~~~~~~~~~~~~~~~~~~~~~~~~

Having completed his Exmoor fishing story, Ian looked around the room and noticed that, despite the late hour and the drinks that had been consumed, not one person was asleep. The attention of each and every one of them was completely upon him. You could have cut the atmosphere with a knife.

"Wow, if you're as good a fisherman as you are a storyteller, then you have a future," Mary said with a yawn. It was way past her bedtime and the drink was having an effect.

"Well that passed the time, didn't it?" he smiled, ignoring her yawn. "I hope I didn't frighten you too much." The remark was addressed to the American party, who were booked to go fishing with him in the morning, and, remarkably, had been stunned into total silence.

"Where are we going tomorrow?" asked one of them

"Clatworthy Lake," Ian replied with a grin. "My French colleague here will start the day by leading us on a walk which will take us above the lake. It's a fantastic view from there. There is an iron-age hill fort on a rocky outcrop above the reservoir. It's roughly triangular in shape and has a single bank, cut through solid rock. There may have been an entrance on the west and two on the east. The ancient settlement of Syndercombe is recorded as held by Turstin FitzRolf. There are seven water inlets at Clatworthy, which are all hot spots for fishermen, but we'll concentrate on the south bank. We should get some Rainbow and Brown Trout."

"Do you fancy joining us?" Philippe asked David and Mary. "It's a beautiful walk."

"I'm sure it is," answered David, "but my heart wouldn't stand it. Besides we're off to follow the Golden Horseshoe."

"Well, never mind. We'll compare notes before dinner tomorrow. I hope you have a good night's rest. I'm looking forward to tomorrow; I'm sure we'll be in good hands," put in one of the transatlantic visitors.

David had a fleeting thought that a good night's rest wasn't the reason for booking The Honeymoon Suite, but that was all that was going to happen. Oh, well, that's life, he thought.

"You won't find better," said Peter as he entered the bar area. He was sweating profusely and had a sticking plaster on one thumb.

"All done, David, Mary, I'm sorry this has happened.  It won't lock tonight, obviously, but that's nothing to worry about." He looked at the assembled throng. "I hope you've not been bored, waiting for me to finish," he said.

"Not at all," said somebody, "your son has entertained us with one of his Exmoor fishing tales. He should be a storyteller on TV."

"I hope it wasn't the one about the little girl who didn't want her father to go fishing," Peter said. "That frightens people every year. It frightens me, and I've heard it more times than I care to remember.  Well, if you'll excuse me, I'm off to have a shower, a drink and bed. It's been a long day and I've got to be up for breakfast."

Everybody said their goodnights and slowly made their way to their respective rooms, each thinking on the Exmoor Fishing Tale and praying for a good night's sleep.

## QUAD BIKES, FAITH AND TRUST

### -20-

There was still more drama to unfold on the night before the fiftieth running of the Golden Horseshoe Challenge. It was as if Exmoor had been waiting all those years just to cram in as much as possible over the two days.

The plan went wrong very quickly. Barry looked in the rear view mirror and didn't see any lights, but he knew they were being pursued and it was only a matter of time before he would see the blue flashes and hear the siren.  He and his younger brother, Tom, fell silent as the tension between them rose.

It was meant to be such an easy job. After all, this was their fifth such robbery and there had been no hiccups so far.  Each Quad Bike had been taken in the dead of night with little or no fuss, and this had followed the same pattern.  They had scoped the farm from afar for a few days, unnoticed up on the moor, and spotted that the bike was stored in a shed near the farm entrance, with only a very inadequate padlock and chain securing the door. They had taken the precaution of spending a whole night there, just to make sure there would be no guard dogs roaming around.  It seemed that this farmer relied on his remote location and a misplaced trust in his fellow man for security, in spite of the local police campaign about valuable machinery being targeted. There had also been no random police patrols on the moor during their surveillance, so they reasoned, quite logically, that it would be an easy job. They had parked the horse box up a lane, out of site of the road leading to the farm, and walked silently. Stopping to make sure all was quiet, Tom cut the chain and padlock and the shed door was opened to reveal their target. The farmer had kindly left its keys hanging on a rail just inside the door. They wheeled the machine out of the shed and replaced the padlock and chain to look as though it had not been touched. The bike was silently pushed up the lane and into the waiting horsebox. Barry and Tom congratulated each other on the smooth operation and the horsebox set out for its destination.

The night was dark with cloud covering the moon and stars, and the wind rustled the leaves with relentless determination. They studied the Exmoor weather carefully before their outings and deliberately chose such nights as they were perfect for their purposes. No rain to muddy the ground and reveal tyre tracks or feet imprints, no light to show their presence and enough wind noise for added cover: perfect on each occasion. Barry had wondered why the police hadn't cottoned on to the conditions on the nights of each robbery, but the sudden appearance of flashing blue in the mirror gave him the answer. Barry knew they could not out run the police car and was desperately looking for a solution.

Tom spotted him first.  A solitary figure stood in the road ahead of the horsebox, flashing a torch and waving for them to stop.  He was not dressed in any uniform and his car was behind him, with its hazard lights flashing. It was obvious that the man was not going to step aside and let them pass, but their own plight was becoming more urgent with every passing second. They had no choice, apart from driving straight over him. Barry slowed to a stop and waited for the man to approach his open window.

"Can you help me?" he asked. "I've swerved to avoid a stag and my car's in the ditch.  Bloody thing just appeared from nowhere. Perhaps you could tow it out. Stupid animal just stared at me and walked away as if it owned the place!"

"Are you hurt?" Barry asked, having observed a trickle of blood from the man's nose.

"No, I don't think so," replied the man. "I just need a pull out of the ditch."

"That's difficult," said Barry, "we're in a bit of a hurry at the moment, but we'll give you a lift and you could come back to fetch your car in the morning."

"I'd rather do it now," persisted the stranger. "I've got other things planned tomorrow."

"That's bad luck," replied Tom, appearing from the rear of the horsebox. He walked towards the man and steadily held a shotgun, pointing it at his midriff. "There's no time to argue."

The blue flashes were getting closer and the brothers knew they were running out of options. Barry jumped down from the driver's seat and they bundled the helpless man into the back of the horsebox, forcing him to sit on the stolen Quad Bike and lashing him there with twine. He was about to have an uncomfortable ride.

"Now what?" exclaimed Tom, as he spotted more lights in the distance ahead.

"We've got to get off this road," said Barry. "They'll squeeze us between them if we don't."

"There's a small track on the right up there," Tom shouted, pointing about fifty yards in front of them. "Turn off the headlights. If we just use sidelights they won't see us turn."

Barry had opened his window and was concentrating on something.

"I said, turn off the lights!" shouted Tom. "They can't see us without lights. What are you doing?" he went on as his brother hung his head out of the window and peered skyward.

"They can find us with those, you know, satellite things." Barry said.

"What are you talking about?"

"You know, they can see us from miles up. I saw it on the telly," said Barry.

"Don't be stupid!" said Tom, losing his patience and pointing again at the right turn. "As long as they haven't got a helicopter up there, we'll be OK."

Barry turned out the headlights and braked hard. There was a muffled cry from behind them in the horsebox from the tethered man.  The vehicle just about made the sharp turn without hitting anything. A large rock appeared in front of them, which reminded Barry of a childhood bad dream in which he had been chased by a spooky weird faced thing that always seemed to catch up with him no matter how fast he ran. He had woken just as he had been caught, but had never forgotten the sweat inducing terror. Many children have such nightmares at some time, but knowing others have them doesn't help. He looked at the rock again and blinked hard to rid himself of the image, as he followed the narrow lane around the rock.

"I know a place down here," said Tom, "it's out of sight of everywhere and we could stay for a couple of days until it's safe. They're only out and about because of that Golden Horseshoe thing.  Once that's over, they'll go back to normal and we'll be able to sort this out."

"Actually, it could help. There'll be so many horseboxes and Quad Bikes around in the morning that they won't know which ones to look at."

"I'm not taking that chance," replied Tom. "Let's get out of sight and give ourselves some time. We need to sort out our friend in the back, anyway."

They found Tom's secret place, parked the horsebox under a canopy of trees and sat in silence for a few minutes, listening intently for any telltale signs of life. Eventually, Tom slipped away into the darkness saying he would only be a few minutes.  Barry locked the door after he had gone, pulled up the collar of his coat and buried himself deep into its folds. The muffled noises from the back had ceased and been replaced by a scraping, shuffling noise. Barry knew he couldn't wait too long before he would have to do something about it. Two police cars raced by, blue lights flashing as they passed the end of the dark lane. Barry realised they must have been close behind, but the winding bends and high hedges had hidden their rear lights.

Tom got into the deserted house by breaking a window in the back. He reappeared and the brothers put a hood over the man's head, before hauling their protesting hostage out of the vehicle and into the house. It was obviously somebody's second home. The fridge was shut off and the phone too, which was a good sign as it showed nobody was intending to return soon. Also, it smelled musty and had stacks of old books and magazines from the previous summer. Tom started to remove the hood.

"What the hell are you doing?" Barry yelled.

"He hasn't said anything," replied Tom, "I was going to make sure he's still OK."

"Leave it on," Barry ordered, "we don't want him to see us any more than is necessary."

Tom shrugged his shoulders and went to the window. He saw another patrol car.  This one passed the end of the lane slowly and appeared to be searching. Barry was pleased they had taken the precaution of not disturbing anything at all which would be visible. They would need to get round the back of the house to see the broken window, and the horsebox was well hidden in its dense thicket.

"Why did you do that?" the voice was muffled from beneath the hood. "Why?" he whispered. He had a low voice and sounded calm.  This seemed unnatural to the brothers, given the situation. They looked at the figure, which by now had been pushed into a chair. He was obviously well muscled and had an easy confidence. His expensively cut suit was dark and he wore no tie. His shoes were of obvious quality.  Barry had been told at some time in his life that you can tell a lot about a person by their shoes and he remembered it now. He was well muscled and seemed to carry himself with an easy confidence, despite his predicament. He was also obviously not local because no local would have been forced off the road by a stag. His face was hidden beneath the hood but Barry remembered it wasn't young; perhaps in his forties and his head was slightly balding.

"Quiet," Tom said. There was another car going by. There were already far too many vehicles for such a time of the night.

The man laughed inside the hood. It was as if he was saying "What? You think they can hear me all the way outside?"

 Barry took it that he was being mocked and didn't like the feeling. "Shut up, I don't want to hear your voice again."

The hooded man eased himself back into the chair with the air of a man who didn't have a care in the world.  He was getting under their skin.

"Why have you got a Quad Bike in the horsebox?  Where's the horse gone?" he asked.

Tom lost his temper. "Quiet!"

"Just tell me why," persisted the man from inside the hood.

"Shut up," roared Tom as he took out his knife and threw it down so that it stuck into a tabletop, with a convincing 'thunk'. "That's an eight inch carbon tempered blade. It would cut clean through any part of you, so be quiet or I might be tempted to use it on you."

Barry was stunned at the outburst.  He was even more amazed when the man in the hood seemed to laugh. It sounded more like a derisive snort really, but it annoyed the brothers.

"Have you got any money on you?" Tom asked and pulled the wallet out of the man's jacket pocket.

"Well, well, well. Look at this," he said as he looked at what must have been five or six hundred pounds fanned out between his fingers and thumbs.

Another police car went past the lane, moving slowly. A siren sounded eerily from far across the moor. Barry took the wallet from Tom and rifled through its contents. He found several copies of the man's business card. Quentin Legard, business and personal contracts. He wondered what that could mean.

"So, Mr Legard, what exactly does business and personal contracts mean?" asked Barry, his mind racing ahead of his mouth as he considered a myriad of possibilities. This man could be valuable.

"I asked you a question, Mr Legard," said Barry.

The man inside the hood breathed easily. He was not stressed and that worried Barry.

"We could hold you for ransom. You must surely be worth a fair amount. Nice clothes, good shoes, expensive car. At least it was until that stag took a disliking to it. Hope you're insured or that will cost a fortune to repair."

"Barry, I want to talk to you," said Tom.

"Shut up!" exclaimed Barry as he bundled his brother out of the room and into the kitchen. "You idiot.  Now he knows my name as well as both our faces. Wonderful! Well done. We start with a simple Quad Bike and we get a smooth businessman.  What a mess. The police are all over the moor and we're trapped here with Mr Quentin Legard.  What sort of name is that anyway?"

"I'm sorry," whined Tom," it just came out. What are we going to do now?"

"I don't know," said Barry, pacing up and down and nagging his fist on the kitchen table. "There's something about him I don't like. He's not scared enough. Any normal person would be shaking and begging to be let go.  All this man does is breath slowly and ask stupid questions.  It's as if he's mocking us."

"So let's teach him a lesson," suggested Tom.

"I told you not to be so stupid," Barry stormed.  Keep calm.  Be rational. There must be a way of turning this to our advantage. We just need to think of it."

"Hello," called Quentin Legard from beneath the hood.

The brothers returned to find him still sitting comfortably, his arms folded, in the same chair.

"My wife and family will be sick with worry," Quentin Legard lied. "Look at their pictures in my wallet."

Barry looked and saw an attractive woman and two perfect children.

"We're not letting you go, just like that," said Barry, "we could demand a ransom for you. There must be half a million in this at least."

"Like a hostage you mean? Asked Legard, "you watch too much TV. You wouldn't get away with it. Just give yourselves up. At least you'll only be facing a theft charge.

"Shut up," shouted Tom, becoming ever more irritated.

"Let me go. I won't say anything against you. Nobody knows I'm here and nobody is looking for me yet. If necessary, I'll tell them you treated me well and I don't wish to press charges. You can disappear with your horsebox and Quad Bike, if you like."

Tom leaned forward and pushed the knife against Legard's throat. He only used the blunt edge because the blade was razor sharp and a mistake was easy to make. "Shut up; now! He ordered."

Barry decided he needed fresh air and took himself off to check around outside.

"Keep an eye on him," he told his brother. "I'm going to take a look round."

Ten minutes later he returned and heard Tom saying, "No way. I'm not handing my brother in."

Barry couldn't believe his ears. Now this man Legard knew his name and the fact that they were brothers. His face mirrored his rage. The situation was rapidly getting out of control.

Tom saw the look and recognised it for what it was. He knew he'd blown it. "He said he'd pay me big money to let him go, but I wasn't going to. I mean we stick together don't we? I wasn't even thinking about it. I told him to forget it. He confused me. I wasn't thinking." Tom's words tumbled uncontrollably.

Barry surprised his brother by clapping him on the shoulder. "It's ok," he said, "it's been a long night. These things happen. Don't worry about it. It'll all be fine in the end. Why don't you spend the night upstairs? I don't want to see you around for a while. I need time to think."

Quentin Legard heard the entire exchange and, waiting until he knew Tom was gone, he sniggered beneath his hood. He was not surprised when Barry removed it and looked into his eyes. "Hello, Barry," Legard smiled. The anger rose in Barry's chest until it almost burst. He moved to the window and looked out. More blue flashes lit the moor, bouncing off the low clouds and the front of the house. "No, Legard said, "it won't work. Ransom, I mean." His eyes were dark and as calm as his breathing and voice.  It angered Barry even more. "I don't have a lot of money," he continued. "The cash in my wallet is about all I could raise, believe it or not.  In my business I have to appear well off; appearances are everything.  People believe what they first see and usually don't think much beyond that. The kids in the picture are long gone now.  That was twelve years ago.  I'm divorced and they're bleeding me dry. Besides, I don't think you could pull it off. You need help, and that brother is hardly professional, is he?"

Barry considered what he had heard. Neither said anything and silence filled the room like it was filling up with cold water. He walked and the floors creaked under his feet, which only made things worse. He recalled his father telling him that a house had a voice of its own and some houses were laughing houses and some were forlorn. This one struck Barry as forlorn.

"I don't want you to kill me," Legard broke into his thoughts.

"Who said I was going to kill you?" replied Barry, taken aback by the question.

Quentin Legard gave a strange smile. "I've been a contractor for over twenty years and I know when somebody is not telling me the truth."

"Tell me why I shouldn't kill you," said Barry surprised at himself for even entering the discussion.

"Oh, I've got several reasons, but there is one in particular," answered Legard.

"You have? And what's that?" asked Barry.

"One that you can't argue with, but I'll get to that in a minute. So let me tell you some of the practical reasons you should let me go. Firstly, you think you've got to kill me because I know who you are. Am I correct? Well, how long do you think your identity is going to be a secret? I don't know much about this sort of thing, but they are bound to gather evidence. You know, tyre marks, witnesses, DNA, CCTV and so on. Even if the horsebox is stolen they will find it and trace it back to you.  They'll find evidence of me having been there, believe me." Legard smiled meaningfully, "and how long will it be before they persuade your brother to say something he doesn't mean to? You know what he's like; he just cannot help himself."

Barry broke. "So, you're saying I'm trapped anyway? If that's the case, I might as well kill you.  Nothing to lose and all that."

"I agree," said Legard. "Go ahead, but I know you don't want to. You're not a murderer. No offence intended, but you're just a small time thief trying to make ends meet and so is your brother. I am right, aren't I?" he went on.

Quentin Legard's eyes bored into Barry like a diamond tipped drill and the latter was lost for words. "I'm going to talk you out of it," Legard affirmed.

"How?" was all Barry could manage.

Legard cleared his throat.  "Could I have some water please?" he asked.

"Of course," Barry replied, "after all, I want to hear this clearly."

Legard took a cultured sip and began. "First, let's get everything on the table. I've seen your face and I know your name. I can describe you accurately, as well as your brother, so you have to assume I can identify you from a picture or anything like that. Here's the rub. My promise is that I will not turn you in. Not under any circumstances. The police will never learn your names from me. I will not give evidence against you. I will not describe you accurately. Also, think about this.  Do you really want to be hunted for murder, when all you've really done is steal some farmer's Quad Bike? I don't even know whether the horsebox is really stolen or whether it's actually yours. Maybe you've had an argument with a local farmer and this is your way of sorting it out. Perhaps you've got some grudge about this Golden Horseshoe thing, I don't know, and I don't want to know. It's none of my business. It's probably better that I don't know."

Barry had to admit that Legard was convincing. He sounded as honest as a priest.

"All I do know," Legard continued, "is that it wouldn't make any sense. It would serve no purpose. There is another reason, though, for me not to say anything about you. You know my name. You have my card and my address. You know I have a family. You know they are important to me because I carry their photos in my wallet. If I turn you in you could come after any of us. I'd never jeopardise my family in that way. Now let me ask you something. What's the worst thing that could happen to you?"

"To have to keep listening to you spout on and on," replied Barry and they both laughed, but Legard pressed the question.

"Seriously? The worst thing? I don't know, I've never thought about it really. Lose a leg? Go deaf? Lose my money? Go blind?" Legard saw that the last thought had hit a nerve.

"Going blind? Yes, I suppose that would be about the worst thing I could think of," replied Barry with feeling, scared by the thought. His father had gone blind in his later years and it had affected Barry greatly. It was having to depend on somebody else for almost everything that really scared him.

"So, think about it this way," Legard said. "The way you feel about going blind is the way my family would feel if they lost me. You don't want to cause them that kind of pain, do you? I don't think you're made that way. I think what's happened tonight has spun out of your control and you don't know what to do."

Barry inwardly admitted to himself that this man was correct on all counts, but didn't want to show weakness. "So what's this last reason you're telling me about?" he said.

"The last reason," Legard whispered, but didn't continue. He gazed around the room with a faraway look in his eyes.

"Yes," pressed Barry, "tell me; convince me." Barry cut the twine that still bound Legard's hands. He didn't believe that Legard would try anything, but remained wary and kept the knife close, ready to be used.

"The last reason?" said Quentin Legard, relaxing in his chair. "I'll tell you. I'll prove to you that you should let me go."

"When?" said Barry, with as much sarcasm as he could muster.

"All those other reasons, the practical ones, the humanitarian ones, I'll concede you don't care much about those. I can see you're not convinced. So, let's look at the one reason you should let me go."

"I wish you would," Barry continued the sarcasm. "Before dawn breaks would be helpful"

"You should let me go for your own sake," stated Legard.

"For my own sake! What on earth are you talking about?" Barry was genuinely confused.

"You see, Barry, I don't think you are totally lost. You're soul's not beyond redemption."

"My soul!" Barry exclaimed. You think I've got a soul?"

"Well, everybody's has a soul," replied Legard. The statement sounded to Barry like the man was surprised that the existence of a soul should be in doubt.

"Well," said Barry after some consideration, "if I've got a soul it's only going to one place."

Legard's concentrated gaze was unsettling Barry, who thought the man was trying to peer right into that very soul. "We're talking about your soul, Barry."

Barry averted his face so that the eye contact was broken.  He felt uncomfortable beneath the penetrating scrutiny.

"I bet you're the sort that goes to church and reads religious stuff," accused Barry, who really didn't know what to say in the circumstances.

"I go to church, but no, I'm not talking about all that 'religious stuff' as you call it. I don't mean magic. I mean your conscience," Legard explained.

"I don't know," was all Barry could muster.

"Not the afterlife," Legard said.  "Not morality. I'm talking about life here on earth and that's important. I really believe if you have a connection with somebody, if you trust them, if you have faith in them, then there's hope for you."

"Hope?"  Barry repeated the word, as if trying to get to grips with a difficult concept. He gave up the struggle and asked, "what's that mean? Hope for what?"

"That you'll become a real human being and lead a real life. Oh, there are reasons to steal and there are reasons to kill. But on the whole, don't you think it's better not to? Just think about it. Why do we put people in jail if it's alright for them to murder? Not just us, but all societies." Quentin Legard was warming to his task.

"So I should give up my evil ways?  Just like that," Barry snapped his fingers to emphasise his point.

"Maybe," Legard said laconically.

Silence insinuated itself between them as they both took stock. Legard was trying to assess his progress whilst Barry wrestled with foreign and difficult concepts.

"My evil ways?" repeated Barry, just to fill the gap whilst he thought of something more meaningful to say.

Legard lifted one eyebrow and said, "maybe. How did you feel when you stole that Quad Bike? How did you feel when you kidnapped me? You knew those things weren't right, didn't you?"

Barry was about to reply, but Legard cut him off. "Don't answer me. You'd only be inclined to lie and that's ok. It's an instinct in your line of work. But I don't want you believing any lies you tell me. I want you to look into your heart and tell me if you don't think something is really wrong about what you and your brother have done. Think about that, Barry. You know something is not right, don't you?"

Barry admitted the errors of his ways to himself, but expressing it was another thing entirely. He wrinkled his forehead as the internal struggle raged, but no matter which way he looked at it the bottom line was about trust. His gut instinct told him so.

"If I let you go, you'll tell them about me. Anybody would. Everybody has, all through my life. Even my father did after he went blind." Barry was near to tears and tried to hide it by turning to the window. He saw more flashing blue lights; sometimes close and sometimes further away across the moor. The night was velvet black and Barry wondered whether that was what it had been like for his father. He hoped not for his sake.

"No I won't," Legard said. "We're talking about an agreement. I'm a contractor, I don't break agreements. I won't tell a soul about you, Barry. I don't break confidences. If you let me go it will make all the difference in the world to you. It'll mean that you're not hopeless. I guarantee your life will be different. That one act, letting me go, will change your life forever. Maybe not this year, or even for five years, but you'll come round. You'll give up stealing, robbing, cheating, abducting people, lying. You know you will."

"Do you expect me to believe that you won't tell anybody?" Barry asked.

"Ah," Legard said, "now we get to the big issue."

"And what's that? Barry asked, fearing the answer.

"Faith," was the only explanation Quentin Legard gave. He fell silent and allowed the weight of the word hang in the room.

A police siren burst into life and shattered the moment.

"Faith is what I'm talking about. A man who has faith is somebody who can be saved.

"Well I don't have any bloody faith," Barry raised his voice.

Quentin Legard was not a man who was easily put off. "If you believe in another human being you have faith."

"Why the hell do you care whether I'm saved or not?"

"Because life is hard and people are cruel. I told you I'm a churchgoer. A lot of the Bible is crazy, but I believe some of it. One of the things I believe is that sometimes we're put in these situations to make a difference. I think that's what has happened tonight.  That's why we're here now. You've felt it, haven't you? Like an omen. It's meant to be. Think about it.," Legard ended.

Barry's face reflected his difficulty.

Legard was talking again and Barry found it hard to concentrate. He thought of himself as a man of action rather than intellectual debate.

"What if everything tonight happened for a reason?  I was driving across the moor and a stag crossed my path. I had to swerve to avoid it and had to flag you down for help. You were going about your lawful business, (sorry, your unlawful business). Surely that's already too many coincidences, isn't it? There's no need for me to go on is there?" Legard asked. He looked at Barry, waiting for a decision. "Also, maybe, just maybe, I've been put here to help you. I'll let you into a secret. I have not always been the honest upstanding citizen you see before you.  I've done my share of things I have come to regret and some I don't. I can't give you details, but they make your little escapade child's play. So perhaps we can both help each other to be better humans."

Barry was lost in thought and silence once again surrounded them. Legard decided not to intrude as he realised that decision time was close for his adversary.

"If I let you go," Barry said quietly, "you'd have to tell them something."

"I'll tell them the truth," Legard replied. "You locked me in the back of the horsebox and tossed me out somewhere near here."

"That's not the truth," said Barry.

"It's near enough," Legard said hastily, not wanting the momentum to be lost. "That's perfectly believable."

"I think you'd flag down a car straight away." Barry was dubious.

"I could," agreed Legard, "but I won't." You don't know for certain, there are no guarantees, so you'll have to have faith."

"If I don't have any faith?" asked Barry.

"Then we're wasting our time even talking," relied Quentin Legard, "and your life will never change. End of story."

Barry walked round the room lost in thought and Legard waited patiently.

"Let me walk outside," suggested Legard.

"Oh yes! Just let you stroll out for some fresh air," said Barry petulantly.

"Here's a proposal," pressed Legard, "let me walk outside and I promise you, I'll walk straight back in again. Think of it as a test."

Barry thought about it for a second. "I'd shoot you in the back with the shotgun if you try to run."

"No!" Legard raised his voice." You put the gun in the kitchen or somewhere else. Anywhere so that you couldn't get it if I ran. You stand by the window, so we can see each other. You've got to assume the worst is going to happen and that if I run I'll tell the police everything and I've got to assume you'll shoot me in the back.  Or we can show trust, show faith in each other."

That word faith again.  It was seeping into Barry's being. He was being shown a different way. "So, you just want me to put the gun down somewhere?"

"Yes.  Let's say the kitchen. Then you just watch me from the front door or the window in this front room.  All I'm going to do is walk outside and get a bit of fresh air. I'll walk, let's say twenty yards down the lane and then turn round and walk right back in." Legard was convincing.

Barry knew that there were bushes on either side of the narrow lane and Legard could take off and not be seen again. He wouldn't be able to get the gun in time and the man knew it. He was being conned.

"No.  No deal. You'll just disappear into thin air and then where would I be?" Barry asked.

Police blue lights continued to flash around the moor and they seemed to be closing in. Barry didn't know what to do. He had never taken a hostage before. He had planned the theft of a Quad Bike and that was all his plan was designed to deal with. The arrival of Quentin Legard was an unwelcome interruption and he was all at sea. The stupid behaviour of his brother Tom had not helped either. On all the TV programmes he had ever seen the captives begged, but this man was different. He was cool, calm and collected. It was as if he knew exactly how to handle the situation and turn the pressure round. Barry recognised his dilemma and knew he had to make a decision.

"No," he said again.

"Ok," said Legard, "at least you thought about it. That's a good thing and I respect that."

Silence returned to the room and Legard sipped some more water. Barry's mind raced and he imagined himself watching television in his own house, with a wife and a couple of children and all the normal things that people have and do. Could he get to that point? He might just get away with theft, but kidnapping and murder were in a different league. Nothing normal happens after those.

"You'd just walk down the lane a bit and then come back?" he asked.

"That's it exactly," responded Legard with a smile. He knew he was winning the psychological battle.  He compared it to negotiating with a sales person.  Once the final figure has been arrived at, the potential buyer has a choice. Either accept it and make a purchase or try a little more. The last thing he should do is to say he'll think about it, and let the sales person know, before walking away. That move stacks the cards heavily in the seller's favour, because if the potential buyer returns the seller knows he has not found a better deal and the price last quoted cannot then be negotiated down.  Legard also knew the value of silence in negotiations, which was why he had allowed it to happen a few times with Barry. Let the other person think; give him time to come round to what you want. Make him believe he is making the decision, whilst the opposite is the case. As soon as he begins to repeat details or ask for confirmation of a point, then you have him.  He can be reeled in.  It was psychological fishing, really. Legard was grateful to his own father for these lessons.  He had accompanied him whenever he was looking for a change of car, for example, and watched carefully as the seller crumbled in front of his eyes. He had not spoken or interrupted either, because that changes the dynamics and allows the seller something else to latch onto. All the fancy lectures and books on technique couldn't hold a candle to his father's skill. They don't teach useful lessons like that in school.

After what he judged to be a suitable time, Legard spoke. "I won't run off; you don't need to get your gun. We trust each other. We each have faith. What could be simpler?"

Barry turned to the window. He listened to the wind, which was not strong but had a steady hiss that he found comforting in a strange way. It was like a voice. He was on the edge and afraid. Finally, he walked over to Legard and pulled him out of his chair. He held the knife to his neck and took him to the front door.

Legard smiled calmly and said, "you're doing a good thing."

Both men smelled cold May night air. There was wood smoke as well and they heard the wind across Exmoor as it lay brooding and waiting for them, as if it knew the endgame was being played out.

"Go on," said Barry, "before I change my mind."

Legard began to walk. He did not look back to check on his adversary. He knew Barry was watching and not looking back showed trust. Barry recognised Legard's faith in him and it gave him hope. Nevertheless he almost panicked and bolted for the gun in the kitchen, but he knew if he did that the man would have disappeared before he got back. Legard walked slowly, testing his man.

A police car's blue lights announced its impending presence and Barry knew it was over. He turned his head, beginning his dash to the kitchen, but was halted by movement in the corner of his eye. He was startled to see Legard bend down and roll underneath a bush, out of site. He closed the door quickly and watched from the darkened front room. A flashlight swept the lane, but didn't locate Legard as he had dug himself deep into the undergrowth. Barry realised with a jolt that he was actually hiding from potential rescue, doing whatever he could to stay out of the way of the light. The car eventually moved on and Barry's eyes searched for Legard. He was amazed when he saw him, large as life, strolling towards him.  Yes, actually strolling rather than walking as though returning from a Sunday lunchtime drink at the local pub. He walked through the front entrance and into the front room. He held out his hands, as if asking for them to be tied again.

Barry was nonplussed. He didn't know how to react, so he just stood there.  He had never before shown anybody such trust and it had been rewarded. Gradually he realised that this man had proved the value of trust and it made him feel good, but it frightened him as well.

"How do you feel?" asked Legard.

It was if this man knew what he was thinking; it was uncanny.

Barry disappeared into the kitchen and returned, not with the gun, but with a bottle of scotch and two glasses. He poured the liquid into both and handed one to Legard.

"Here's to faith," said Legard and raised the glass to his lips.

"To trust," replied Barry, taking a sip as he turned to look out of the window. He considered the vast moor beyond and was glad to be inside the house. It was a good feeling; a real thing, however small. It was a beginning. He took another sip.

"Pour us another," Legard said and Barry filled the glasses to the top. "Here's to you," Legard continued.

"And you," said Barry, raising his glass. Having taken a gulp, he lowered the glass to look at the man standing in front of him. "I'm glad it's turned out like this," he said raising his glass once more, before lowering his head to take a larger gulp.

It happened at that precise moment. Barry felt a stinging sensation as whisky was thrown into his eyes and he howled in pain. He sniffed through his nose and rubbed feverishly at the burning. Legard brought his knee up into his chin and knocked out a couple of teeth in the process. Barry fell backwards to the floor and Legard dropped onto his stomach, again using his knee. The wind left Barry with a huge rushing sound and he was paralysed, hardly able to breathe. The pain was incredible. He couldn't see anything and neither could he hear properly as his ears were roaring inside his head. Before he was able to react his hands were tightly bound with twine and he was being pulled onto a chair and his legs similarly treated.  He felt his legs being tied and vaguely heard the creak of footsteps on the stairs before he passed out.

Legard threw water at Barry's face to wash the whisky from his eyes and stood before him, waiting patiently, staring at his foe. He was not smiling and his whole demeanour had changed. Barry eventually recovered enough wind to let out a gasp and managed to open his eyes. He saw Legard taking another sip of his whisky.

"I was going to let you go," he panted. "I trusted you." His mental anguish was almost equal to his physical pain. "You said you weren't going to turn me in!"

"You can shout all you like, nobody will hear you.  You can't wake your brother," said Quentin Legard, "I wasn't going to turn you in. Let me explain. It wasn't coincidence that I flagged you down tonight.  There was no stag and my car is in perfect condition.  Those photos in the wallet were not of my family.  The money was a trap. You saw it and got greedy.  You thought there would be more to be had. There is, actually, but you'll never see it."

Barry's face was a study in confusion.

"You still don't understand, do you? Legard continued. You've been stealing Quad Bikes and other machinery for some time, haven't you?  The farmers here on Exmoor got together and hired me to help them.  You see, I was telling the truth. My business card says that I am a business and personal contractor. It simply fails to mention what type of contract I undertake.  This is business for me, but it's personal for my clients. Oh, by the way, I gave you my word and will keep it; I won't go the police. Turning you in is the last thing I want to do."

"Then what do you want?" trembled Barry as the hopelessness of his predicament sank in.

"My clients want their goods back; it's simple. Once we've managed that, well who knows?" said Legard as he reached for Barry's sharp knife.

"What are you going to do?" yelled Barry, ashen faced and shaking uncontrollably.

"Well, I'll tell you, "said Legard. " After we've recovered every single item that you and your brother have stolen, and it won't take long for you to tell me where they are, we are going to go over our conversation tonight. I spent a great deal of time proving to you that you shouldn't kill me. Now I'm going to spend a great deal of time proving to you that you should have. You see, it's become a personal contract for me as well. Well, I say 'see'; but you may not shortly."

Quentin Legard approached his erstwhile captor, smiling.

## THE FIRST DAY

### -21-

None of the competitors were aware of the dramatic events concerning the recovery of the Golden Horseshoe and the Quad Bikes as they made their way to the gathering point on the first morning of the challenge. The Ride venue (Exford Show Field) is situated on the B3223, just south of Exford, marked on the OS map no 181, as Hernes Barrow (Grid ref.852369). This superb venue, with space for parking, warming-up, marquees, trade stands and arena displays, allows almost instant access to open moorland, with very little roadwork, and a gentle start (although not such a gentle finish) for the Golden Horseshoe Ride.

Exmoor National Park contains a variety of magnificent landscapes and the central plateau of open moorland is remote and spacious. To the north the moorland terminates in towering cliffs above the Bristol Channel. Rocky headlands, steep wooded ravines, plunging waterfalls and jumbled heaps of fallen rock make this an area of outstanding scenic beauty; it is defined as a Heritage Coast.

Inland, the grass moorland is surrounded by heather-clad rounded hills mostly over 300 m (900ft). Dunkery Beacon is the highest point on Exmoor 519 m (1704 ft).

Exmoor was in one if its benign moods. It was a beautiful, crystal clear mid May morning as the riders, their horses and support teams gathered for the fiftieth running of the Golden Horseshoe, the premier endurance event in the country. With a long equine history there was no more appropriate location. The 267 square miles of the National Park boasts stunning landscapes and views, but the competitors, whilst aware of the special nature of the Moor, would not have time to linger and take it all in.  There was an average speed time limit for each class in the competition, and they were not easy to achieve.

Tamsyn Carter had entered the most difficult class of all, The Exmoor Golden Horseshoe Ride, which required her horse, Dobbin, to carry her over approximately 80 kilometres on each of two consecutive days. They would need to average a minimum of 9.5kph in order to avoid elimination and win a Bronze Award. If they wanted to qualify for a Silver Award their speed would need to be between 10.5 and 12kph, whilst the requirement for a Gold Award was to average at least 12kph. Their route on the first day would include parts of the track and trail from Nether Stowey to Lynmouth, across Somerset's wildest landscape. It would take in places which inspired Samuel Taylor Coleridge, William and Dorothy Wordsworth to lay the seeds of Romantic Poetry some 200 years ago. The second day would see them following an equally demanding route back to Exford, passing close to Porlock and taking in the Vale of Porlock.

For Karen Wilson it was her first experience of the event, and she had chosen to enter The Exmoor Experience, which was a ride of 80km, divided equally over two days. This demanded her borrowed horse to transport her over the distance at the same average speeds.

There was also a system of penalties which both would have to avoid. The minimum speed for completion was 9.5kph and had to be maintained each day. The first heart rate reading (i.e. before the trot up) taken at the end of each day was be used as the basis for the awarding of penalty points. Finally, penalty points could be incurred for heart rate only, with the award gained being dropped by one place for such a penalty. It was not for nothing that it had become known as the toughest equine endurance event in the country.

Riders were recommended to carry emergency first aid kits comprising triangular bandage, whistle, glucose tablets, space blanket, wound dressing and bandage and vet wrap type bandage. Riders also had to have a support crew, and there were rules for them as well. They had to be over 17 years of age, named on the entry form, (max one vehicle only per competitor) and able to arrange collection of the horse from the course if necessary.  No horse boxes were permitted to be used to crew.

As this was the fiftieth running of the event, the equine fraternity had responded magnificently. There were record numbers entered in the various classes, so the moor would echo to the sound of hooves for the next two days. The competitors followed designated routes which were traced in coloured lines on Ordnance Survey maps, each colour indicating the route for a particular class. They were to travel over moorland, through woods, along the odd narrow lane, splash through water of varying depths and hurry along pathways.

The routes were physically marked by signposts bearing sponsors' details, at not inconsiderable cost to each. For the riders these took priority over the normal Exmoor wooden signposts, which indicate permitted routes with yellow, blue and purple arrows. Whichever class had been entered, each route would take the rider across high moorland, through deep and wooded valleys and some wonderfully remote and tranquil places. One particular highlight was a bluebell pathway on the way to Withypool that all categories had to use. It was escapism, a journey through time, combined with the edge of competition; an adrenalin filled challenge that tested horse and rider to the limit.

The weather was glorious for the first day, which meant hydration would need to be considered carefully, as well the dangers of sunburn. All entries, whatever the class, had to be recorded in a log. This noted the rider's name, the name of the horse and the crew's details. For most this was done online and the number of postal entries had been falling in recent years. The five entrants for the Golden Horseshoe category, including Tamsyn and her horse, Dobbin, set out at 7.30am and returned to the venue for their halfway vetting just after 10.30. They had a fifty minute hold before being checked by the vet just before setting out again.

The Exmoor Experience was the most popular category. Earlier that morning, the Exmoor Experience entrants, including Karen Wilson, were trotted up at 10am and pronounced fit to start. Lisa

Richards, now without a husband and supported by a crew of four friends, arrived on Monty, full of expectation and barely able to contain her excitement at such a new experience. Karen and Lisa struck up an immediate friendship and spent the day riding together. Also among their number was a Mr T F Fag, riding a horse named Gus ESM.

Karen Wilson was in particularly fine form, and had a glorious day's ride.  She finished well within the permitted average time and was on course for a Gold Award. Her horse had performed brilliantly and was safely tucked in for the night in the adjoining stables. Her husband, Kevin, was particularly proud of Karen that day. He had followed them on their journey and the exhilaration of chasing them from one place to the next had made him forget his own difficulties. His friends had supported them magnificently. He knew that she had found something that would see her though their dark days that both knew were not far ahead. He was thankful that she could now turn to something when he was gone, and it made him tearful with gratitude. He was, however, determined not to display his feelings until she had completed the challenge.  He had made plans, saved money, and his time was near. He planned to buy the pony she had borrowed for the event, as well as a horsebox and a four by four to pull it.  He had already paid for a year's livery at a local stables.  The whole thing cost him a small fortune, but he reasoned that he couldn't take it with him and the idea was for his wife to support their charity via her equine activities.  He knew she would be good enough to compete at a high level and it was a burning ambition within her. Kevin was pleased he was able to deliver such a present to his wife. She deserved much more; so much more, and he could provide more in death than he could ever give her in life.  He tried to verbalise his feelings but could only say that he was proud of her and she deserved all he could provide.

That evening at the bar of the crowded Exmoor White Horse Inn, the halfway standings were announced. In The Golden Horseshoe category two riders were on Bronze speed, one was on Silver and Tamsyn was on Gold speed. Unfortunately, one had retired with a lame mount. In the very popular Exmoor Experience class there were 7 Bronze, seven Silver, including Lisa, and 18 Gold, including Karen Wilson, with only one elimination, due to a rider having fallen and hurt her back. Lisa and Monty had only missed the Gold speed time by a small margin and were determined to put that right the next day.

After the standings had been made public, Karen told Kevin and her team about a strange occurrence.

"I'm a bit worried about the horse we borrowed for this," she said. "As you know I've been training with him for The Exmoor Experience for quite a while, getting ready for the big competition and about two weeks ago I was riding in the early evening in the ménage at the stables where he is kept. The ménage is flat, floodlit and overlooks two fields from the next farm and two of the fields where the horse is kept. I was the only rider in the ménage, and as soon as I entered the gate the horse started playing up. He was rearing, running sideways and was really spooked. It got worse when got to the far right hand corner which overlooks the next farm's field. I looked and saw a strawberry or grey horse with a rider in dark clothes, who appeared to be walking down a track between two of the fields.

I pushed my horse forward and whispered to him to calm down, but he started again as soon as we got to the next corner. This time it was worse. He was snorting and sweating. When I looked to see if the horse and rider were scaring him, they were at the bottom of the field. There was no way they could have gone that distance in that time. It didn't stop there. Every time I turned the figure had moved huge distances that no horse could have galloped. I suddenly realised that this horse and rider were not making any noise, and, strangely, were riding in a pitch black field. I only saw them once again and then the vision vanished.

I decided to give my horse time to settle so I turned him out. He usually hates coming in from the field, but had only been turned out for about twenty minutes when a girl, who was bringing in her own horse, told me that my horse was going crazy, trying to jump the fence and looking terrified. I ran down the field and he almost jumped the gate and was galloping around looking scared witless. I finally calmed him down and put him in his stables. I told the story to another girl at the farm and she asked me to show her the track I had seen the horse and rider on. She said she didn't think there was even a track there. The following day I took her to the ménage in daylight and pointed at the track. Apparently it had been out of use for about two years and was so overgrown that even a tractor would struggle to get down it.

As if all that is not strange enough, I swear I saw the same rider and horse today on the moor. They were using a track which other people say is not there. I can't explain it, but there's definitely something odd going on. Thankfully, my horse didn't get spooked today and we completed the course without any trouble, but I'm worried about tomorrow. I think I'll latch on to another rider or two and go round with them."

Karen finished her story and took a large gulp from her glass. She was obviously shaken and was trembling slightly.

"Good idea," said Kevin, "and we'll keep a wary eye out as well. I wonder whether anybody has reported anything.  It's strange, though, that you should see them here and at home. It's hundreds of miles away. We should ask in the morning before you set off. Perhaps I'll speak to somebody while the vet is giving the horse the once over."

At another table in the bar area Tamsyn was reliving her day. David Trent and his wife, Mary had joined them for drinks before dinner.

"It was difficult, very difficult," she said. "We've trained well for this, but it's even harder than I thought. I know we've managed the time and Dobbin has been passed fit, but I ache all over and I'm sore in some unmentionable places.  I hope I'll feel more like it after a good night's rest. Today has made me realise that this is proper endurance, not just a race over flat countryside. I know it's been sunny, but it's still a battle with the elements. I now understand what it takes to cope with Exmoor, even on a good day."

# THE SECOND DAY

## -22-

Exmoor woke on the morning of Day Two to the sound of sharp showers. There was bright sunshine between them, but parts of the moor remained wet. By the time the five Golden Horseshoe riders set out for their second day at around 8am, the moor was again looking glorious.

At the venue, there was general surprise at the sight of a line of Quad Bikes. They had obviously been cleaned and polished and were gleaming in the early morning sunshine. A smiling Quentin Legard, who had managed hardly any sleep at all, stood with two sorry looking, dishevelled characters in the midst of a huddle of local farmers. The media were already sniffing around and taking the pictures which would go with their reports. The two thieves, who both sported bandages and dark glasses, had been forced to clean the Quad Bikes, and were now being made to apologise to each and every owner in turn. There was a uniformed police presence at the venue, but they were showing no interest in the Quad Bike action. Only one sharp eyed person in the crowd noticed two men in the background, standing with their arms folded and conversing with nobody. They made sure they did not appear in any pictures as they soaked up the scene for later scrutiny.

Despite having been granted a day's leave, PC Tony Walker was also present at the venue for the start of Day Two, though not, of course, in uniform.  He had ceremonially hung that in a suit carrier inside his wardrobe when he arrived home the previous night. He wandered amongst the people, receiving nods and greetings, getting used to life as a plain clothes officer.  He felt somehow liberated, free from the restriction that his uniform brought, but he realised that with that freedom came responsibility. They say (whoever 'they' are) that a policeman is never off duty and it was certainly true in his case. He was determined to make an impression in his new role, even if his methods were a little unorthodox. His were the first pair of sharp eyes to spot the two strangers.

Lisa Richards also had sharp eyes but she did not spot the two strangers.  Her attention was caught by the unexpected sight of Quentin Legard. She wondered what nefarious contract he was engaged upon that day, and whether he would still be around at the end of her day's ride. She didn't have time to dwell on him, however, because she and Karen were about to start and she wanted to do well enough to gain the Gold speed standard, both for herself, and to help Karen maintain her position as well. Lisa needed to make up about fifteen seconds to turn her Silver into Gold and they would ride together again with those aims binding them.

Things turn out for the best if you are a glass half full person. Both Karen and her new friend Lisa followed that philosophy, which was just as well because it helped them cope with the day's events. The weather was glorious as the competitors in the Exmoor Experience category set out for their second day at 10.30am and Lisa and Karen settled to a decent pace as the field began to spread out. They had calculated how quickly they needed to travel to achieve their times and set out a schedule which their crews would check at each checkpoint and watering/feeding station. They were ahead of time after the third check, so felt relaxed and comfortable as they approached Tarr Steps.

This is a seventeen span clapper bridge which is made of un-mortared stone slabs and spans the River Barle. It is 180 feet and is the longest of its kind in Great Britain. It was first mentioned in Tudor times but may be much older, possibly even dating back to around 1000BC. The river has silted up over the last century and often comes over the stones in times of flood. The bridge has had to be repaired several times as stones of two tonnes have been washed up to 50 metres downstream. The last occasion was in December 2012, when half of the bridge fell victim to the swollen river. It has since been repaired, with the stones being numbered for easy replacement.

According to local legend, the stones were placed there by the Devil to win a bet, and he still has sunbathing rights on its stones. The myth says that the devil swore he would kill anyone who tried to cross his bridge. The terrified locals got the parson to face him. A cat was sent over the Bridge but was vaporised in a puff of smoke. The parson then set off and met the Devil midway. The Devil swore and intimidated him but the parson reciprocated equally and finally the Devil conceded to let people pass except when he wants to sunbathe.

The woodlands around Tarr Steps is particularly beautiful and are internationally significant for the mosses, liverworts and lichens, including a type of moss found in burrows, which appears to glow in the dark.  Dormice live amongst the hazel, blackberry and honeysuckle and otters feed on fish and eels.

Spectators watched from the nearby Jubilee Trail as the competitors tackled this section of the route that took in Tarr Steps and the area surrounding Hawkridge and Dulverton. Winsford Hill and South Hill were also on the route where the free living Anchor herd of Exmoor ponies could be spotted. These ponies are thought to be a race of wild horse rather than a breed.

Lisa and Karen had no time to appreciate their surroundings as they pressed ahead. They took their horses splashing through the River Barle at Tarr Steps.  Their mounts seemed to thoroughly enjoy the coolness and seemed stimulated.

Lisa looked in front and could not believe her eyes. There, in full view of them both, was an empty stagecoach. She called out to her friend, "do you see it?"

"My God!" exclaimed Karen as the two women tried to control their mounts, which by now were spooked and very skittish.

"What the hell?" asked Lisa.

"I don't know," gasped Karen.

Both fought to control their mounts and looked away.  When they looked again it was gone and their horses had calmed down.

"Did you see it?" called Lisa to a spectator.

"See what?" she asked.

"A stagecoach; there, in the water in front of us."

"I'm sorry, there's nothing there," somebody called, and others confirmed that the two riders were imagining things.

"Maybe the sun's got to you," another person shouted.

"Come on," Karen cried, "I don't like it here.  Let's get going." She squeezed her legs and the horse responded so quickly that Lisa had give Monty a dig in the ribs to spur him and try to catch up.

They rode the rest of the course in virtual silence, each contemplating what they had witnessed.  They completed the challenge in a far quicker time than expected as they raced to leave the apparition behind. Both easily achieved the Gold Speed target, but their mounts had reached the limit of their endurance. Thankfully, both were passed fit by the vet, so their awards were guaranteed.

Prize Giving was scheduled for 7pm, so Lisa, her crew, Karen, Kevin and her crew all met in the bar of The White Horse an hour before that. They also booked a table for dinner in the restaurant for later. They were sitting quietly going over the day together.  All were tired but elated. Karen had told her new friend about Kevin's illness during the ride and Lisa was full of respect for them both.

For her part, Lisa told Karen about her husband's waywardness. She omitted to mention that she had arranged to have him killed, preferring to say that he had been lost at sea just prior to the Horseshoe. They felt a mutual bond. Lisa was recently widowed and Karen was soon to join her. They had found comfort in adversity, and they would go on to become firm friends, meeting up whenever they could, and at the very least making Exmoor in May an annual event for them. Kevin was comforted that his wife was beginning to move on and was not in the least upset that it was happening before his passing.

Tamsyn, together with her daughter Katie and David and Mary Trent, sat at an adjoining table. She was exhausted, having successfully completed the most difficult challenge, The Exmoor Golden Horseshoe itself. By the end of the course her mount, Dobbin, was out on his feet and the vet only passed him at the second attempt. David and Mary had spent the morning following Tamsyn's progress, driving rapidly to and fro across the Moor. They had spent the afternoon in The Honeymoon Suite, with its newly fixed and lockable door. They were as tired as most of the occupants of the bar, but not for the same reason, and had enjoyed the day hugely.

"Did you hear that?" asked David, looking around his table.

"You're not being nosy again, are you?" asked Mary. "It'll get you in trouble one day, you know."

David ignored her jibe and lowered his voice. "The people on the next table are talking about that stagecoach. They saw it as well."

He glanced across at Lisa and Karen's table. "Have you had a good day?" he asked.

"Excellent," replied Karen. "We both managed to get the Gold time, so it's champagne with the meal tonight. How about you?"

"Yes, me too," Tamsyn beamed. "I'm absolutely worn out, but what a day!"

"I couldn't help hearing, please don't think me rude," David said, "but you were talking about seeing a stagecoach out there today."

"Yes, we both saw it at Tarr Steps. We couldn't believe our eyes, but there it was. I'm sure it was real, but some spectators said they didn't see anything," Karen said.

"That's where I saw it too!" Tamsyn cried. "I was on my own so nobody will believe me."

"Oh, it was real enough."

All the occupants of both tables turned their heads towards a man, leaning against the bar. He was tall, pretty well built and slightly balding. His was dressed in casual but smart attire, which was well cut and obviously expensive. There was an authority about him that demanded attention. Some people have that quality. Lisa drew a sharp intake of breath and her face drained of colour, but nobody noticed.

"I don't wish to intrude. You obviously have a good deal to celebrate, but if you'll allow me, I'll tell you about it. It will take a few minutes, so I hope you all have fresh drinks."

The stranger pulled up a chair and sat himself at the head of the table, next to Lisa. Their thighs rubbed and she moved aside as unobtrusively as she could, knowing her face was now colouring rapidly.

"The stagecoach you saw, and believe me you did see it, was being used to transport a highwayman to his execution. You have all heard of or read R D Blackmore's Doone saga. Well, one of the characters in it was Tom Faggus, who was born in North Molton and was a respected landowner. He earned his living as a blacksmith. He was due to marry a local girl and a few weeks before the wedding he won a gold Jacobus for the best shod horse in North Devon. This was an English gold coin of the reign of James I. This caused so much jealousy among some people that they conspired to use the intricacies of the law courts to cheat him out of his land and smithy, and succeeded. Upset, Tom went to see his girl-friend who promptly cold-shouldered him now that he was penniless. This made him so bitter that he vowed he would make the world pay for his maltreatment.

He became a highwayman. During his long career, which lasted from about 1650 until 1671, he preyed upon stagecoaches which the wealthy used to travel to and from the West Country. During his successful career he had several narrow escapes from the lawmen, but there is no record that he killed anyone. He set himself apart from other robbers by treating his victims with great courtesy and was not violent, unlike others. He also notably only stole from the very wealthy and left the poorer folk alone. He was known to be generous to the poor.

.As with Dick Turpin's horse, Tom's horse is legendary and was known as the "Enchanted Strawberry Mare". He found her as a foal, near to death in a muddy pond and nursed her back to health. Her fleetness of hoof was a marvel, and when in danger, she would get her master out of trouble using tooth and hoofs. It is said that on one occasion, Faggus was recognized in Barnstaple and was chased as far as Barnstaple's famous long bridge. When he was half-way across constables appeared at both ends. Seeing his chances of escape rapidly dwindling, Faggus and his mare jumped clear and swam to safety. At the scene of this remarkable escape, Barnstaple Bridge crosses a tidal estuary, the water being some forty feet below the parapet.

On another occasion, information leaked out that Faggus was heading for Exford, and the authorities placed men in different parts of the village to 'ensure' that they caught him. Faggus heard of these plans and later rode boldly into the place in disguise. Seeing the crowd he called:

"Pray my good friends, for what purpose are you waiting here in such numbers?"

On being told that they were waiting for the villain Faggus, he promptly offered to join in and help them in their quest. After a while, he asked them what firearms they had available and suggested that, since the morning was very damp and the priming would be too damp to work, the weapons should be discharged and reloaded. His companions agreed. Immediately they had done so, Faggus drew his pistols! With the crowd disarmed, he had the situation in his own hands and promptly proceeded to rob them of anything of value before galloping away!

At a later date, Faggus' mare is reputed to have again helped her master with more than human intelligence. He was suddenly overpowered when drinking in an alehouse in Simonsbath. Whistling loudly with his accustomed call, he attracted the attention of his mare which was waiting outside. In she rushed, kicking and biting at her master's assailants, whereupon Faggus jumped on her back and made good their escape!

Legends abound concerning Faggus and his mare. What finally and truthfully happened to Tom is uncertain. Legend has it that he was captured by a trap set for him in 1671. In a tavern, a constable dressed as a beggar was offered a drink by Tom. The beggar knocked Tom to the ground and bound him. Tom tried to whistle for his mare, but the horse had been killed in the stable.

He was sentenced to hang in a town in Somerset but there is no record of his execution. Some say the stagecoach that transported him never got to the town and that Tom Faggus may have escaped. Legend says his spirit is often riding Exmoor on his magical strawberry mare.

He was immortalised in R D Blackmore's book "Lorna Doone" as a character who married John Ridd's sister and who obtained a pardon from King James II.

I think the stagecoach you saw was the one that was being used to transport him to his execution. It was empty because he escaped."

The stranger completed his tale and reached for his glass. Lisa risked a glance sideways and Quentin Legard favoured her with a smile as he set his glass back on the table. He took a chance and gently pressed his thigh against hers under the table. He was both surprised and pleased when she reciprocated. The others knew nothing of the nascent relationship and Lisa preferred to keep it that way.  She didn't understand why she found the man quite so interesting, but she didn't seem to be able to help herself. Perhaps it was the danger, she thought.  For he certainly represented danger, from what she knew about him.

They became aware of two men with northern dialects, standing nearby. The first man, Dennis, was relating a story to the other.

"It's an odd case," he said loudly enough to be heard above the increasing volume of chatter in the bar. "We've only been here a few days and already we've uncovered some pretty unsavoury people, as well as some pillars of the community. There's nothing to charge anybody with at the moment, but it's a good example of revenge. We'll have to see how it pans out, but I think there's more to it than meets the eye. You know the beautiful house we passed just outside the village, there's a story behind it. The owner and his wife came to the end of their relationship and eventually they divorced. This bloke spent the first day following his divorce packing his belongings into boxes, crates and suitcases. On the second day, he had the removal company collect his things. On the third day, he sat down for the last time at their beautiful dining room table by candle-light, put on some soft background music, and feasted on a kilo of Tiger prawns, a jar of caviar, and a bottle of spring-water. When he had finished, he went into each and every room and deposited a few half-eaten shrimp shells dipped in caviar into the hollow of the curtain rods. He then cleaned up the kitchen and left.

His ex and her new partner had stayed here at The White Horse while they waited for him to move out. I wonder which room they stayed in? Perhaps that's something for us to look at as well.

When his ex returned with her new partner, all was bliss for the first few days. Then slowly, the house began to smell. They tried everything; cleaning, mopping and airing the place out. Vents were checked for dead rats and carpets were steam cleaned. Air fresheners were hung everywhere. Exterminators were brought in to set off gas canisters, during which they had to move out for a few days and in the end they even paid to replace the expensive wool carpeting. Nothing worked!! People stopped coming over to visit. Repairmen refused to work in the house. The maid quit. Finally, they could not take the stench any longer and decided to move. A month later, even though they had cut their price in half, they could not find a buyer for their stinky house. Word got out and eventually even the local estate agents refused to return their calls. Finally, they had to borrow a huge sum of money from the bank to purchase a new place. The ex called and asked her how things were going. She told him the saga of the rotting house. He listened politely and said that he missed his old home terribly and asked if they would be willing to reduce their divorce settlement in exchange for getting the house. Knowing he had no idea how bad the smell was, they agreed on a price that was about 1/10th of what the house had been worth, but only if he were to sign the papers that very day. He agreed and within the hour his lawyers delivered the paperwork. A week later the ex and her partner stood smiling as they watched the moving company pack everything to take to their new home. And just to spite her ex-husband, they even took the curtain rods!!!"

"Now that's what I call revenge. I wish I had thought of that," said Vince as both men laughed.

They moved away from the table in order to be out of earshot.

"Do you think they picked up the reference to it being an odd case?" said Vince to Dennis

"I hope so," replied Dennis. "Now let's see what effect it has."

# THE EXMOOR STALKER

## -23-

The divorced wife and the new love of her life, having moved out of the smelly house, set up home about five miles away in a remote part of the Moor. They hoped for a peaceful new life; a new beginning. Gwen had even purchased a pony and entered The Golden Horseshoe in an attempt to find new friends and become part of the community. She was really a novice and hadn't had time to do much training, so she sensibly entered the least taxing of the categories. What training she had undertaken had been curtailed by her conviction that she was being stalked.

"I think he's out there, again," Gwen screamed. She was at the kitchen window and let a dish fall and shatter.

"Come away from the window," Trevor ordered.

Gwen didn't, couldn't move. "How can he be there? They promised six months at least."

Trevor peered through the living room curtains, squinting and his heart sank. "It's him," he sighed. "It's him. I'll call the police," Trevor shouted, "and get away from that window. I don't want him to see you."

He stabbed one speed dial button and stared outside with the phone clamped to the side of his head. He moved to the back door, opened it and stepped out. He wanted the stalker to see the phone being held to his ear. He was struck by the peaceful beauty of the surrounding Moor on this cool May evening. They had moved there to find peace and get away from her vindictive ex husband and thought they were settling to a blissful untroubled existence. The night found the Moor calm, inviting and there was the beginning of a mist in the air.  And it found the brooding form of a man crouching in the bushes staring into their bedroom window.

Oh dear Lord, Trevor thought hopelessly. Not again. It's not starting again. The phone clicked and he asked for PC Tony Walker. As he waited to be connected, he inhaled the stale, metallic scent of the metallic porch post he was resting his head against. He looked across his garden and estimated forty yards to the bush that had become a fixture in his daydreams and the focus of his nightmares. It was beside this bush that the man had spent much of the last eight months, in his particular stance, stalking Gwen.

"How did he get out?" Gwen wondered. "I don't see what good it'll do, " Gwen said from the kitchen, panic in her voice, "to call the police. He'll be gone before they get here. He always is."

"Please, get away from the window," Trevor called. "Don't let him see you." The thin blonde woman, her face as beautiful as Lladro porcelain, backed away.

"I'm scared." She had been tall and muscular in her youth, exuding the confidence of the competitive athlete she'd been in her twenties, but she had changed completely as a result of her marriage.

"'Don't worry, dear, you're safe. He's not going to hurt you while I'm here."

Gwen nodded uncertainly and moved away from the window. Trevor kept his gaze coldly fixed on the figure next to the bush. It was a cruel irony that this was happening to Gwen. Conservative by nature, Trevor had always been horrified by the neglect he saw on the part of families in the city to which he commuted every day. Absent fathers, crack-addict mothers, abusive husbands, gangs, women turning to prostitution to feed their habit. He vowed that nothing bad would ever happen to Gwen. His plan was simple: he'd protect Gwen, give her the life she hadn't yet been able to have. He'd keep her close to home. It was for him serious work, but he was already seeing the results. Gwen was gradually relaxing and coming out of herself. He knew the Moor was an integral part of the strategy and so he felt it unfair that it was now party to concealing the stalker.

It had begun last autumn. One evening Gwen had been particularly quiet throughout the evening meal. Trevor asked her to find a book for him in his study because he knew she had put it there the day before, but she hadn't responded. Gwen just stood at the kitchen window, staring outside.

"Gwen? Are you OK?"

She'd turned and to his shock he saw she was crying. "Oh, I'm sorry,' Trevor had said automatically and stepped forward to put his arm around her. He knew the problem. Several days ago she'd had a fall whilst riding on the Moor and it had shaken her badly. He thought it had shaken her too badly to have just been a simple fall. She'd fallen into his arms, sobbing. He was filled with overwhelming love and an unbearable agony for her obvious pain.

"'What is it, darling? Tell me. You can tell me anything."

She'd glanced out the window. Following her gaze, he'd seen a figure standing slightly bent forward in the bushes.

"Oh, Trevor, he's following me."

Horrified, Trevor had led her to the living room. "What is it, my love? Tell me."

That autumn night Gwen had sat with her hands in her lap, staring at the floor, and explained in a meek voice, "I was out riding, and there was this man."

Trevor's heart had gone cold, hands shaking, and anger growing within him. "What happened?" "Nothing happened. Not like that. He just like started to talk to me. He's said 'you're so pretty. I'll bet you're smart. Where do you live?'

"Did he know you?" Did you know him?"

"No, to both questions. He acted all funny, like he was sort of retarded, you know. Kind of saying things that didn't make sense. I told him I don't usually talk to strangers and rode home as fast as the horse would take me. I didn't think he followed me. But..." She bit her lip, "But that's him."

Trevor had jogged toward the bush where he'd seen the man. He was in a curious pose that reminded him of a highwayman, standing with his pistols held at the ready. He saw Trevor approaching and fled.

Police Constable Tony Walker knew all about the man, or thought he did. As a local bobby it was his job to know his patch and the people within it. He knew Gwen's ex husband was of average intelligence and had suffered psychotic episodes when younger. The police hadn't been able to stop him because he'd only hurt one person in all his months of stalking. The girl's brother had attacked him and been almost beaten to death for his trouble. All charges had been dropped on grounds of self defence. Since the divorce a man had taken to stalking Gwen and everybody assumed it was her ex husband. Trevor had tried to obtain an injunction, preventing him coming within a mile of Gwen, but the magistrate didn't play ball. Finally, after the man had stationed himself beside the bush for six consecutive nights, Trevor stormed into his solicitor's office and demanded action. Nothing was done and now he was back, standing highwayman erect with pistols at the ready.

Finally PC Walker came on the line, "Trevor, I was going to call you."

"You knew about him!" Trevor shouted, "why the hell didn't you tell us? He's out there right now."

"What about my Gwen?" he continued shouting. "What are we going to do? More to the point, what are you going to do about this?" Trevor spat the words.

"There's nothing I can do," PC Walker replied. "I'll get your place watched and we'll get him if he does anything. There's no law against somebody standing beside a bush on the Moor."

"But he's watching her; he's stalking her." Trevor was exasperated.

"As I say, I'll get extra random patrols out. I must warn you, Trevor, don't do anything. Just call us if anything happens. Don't take it into your own hands. It will get very complicated if you do."

Tonight as the mist settled over Exmoor on a beautiful May night, the man was frozen in his familiar pose, dark eyes searching for a delicate young woman whose partner happened to be deciding at that moment that this couldn't go on any longer.

"Look Trevor, I know it's difficult," PC Walker said sympathetically, "But you must let us handle it." Trevor slammed the phone down, nearly smashing into a thousand pieces.

"Trevor, please," Gwen began.

He ignored her and as he started for the door she took his arm. She was a strong woman, but Trevor was stronger and he pulled away brusquely. He pushed open the back door and started across the dewy lawn. To his surprise, and pleasure, the man didn't flee. He stood there and crossed his arms, waiting for Trevor to approach. Trevor was athletic. He played tennis and golf and he swam like a fish. He was slightly shorter than his foe, but as he gazed at the man's prominent eyebrows and disturbingly deep-set eyes, he knew in his heart that he could crush him with his bare hands if he had to.  All he needed was the slightest provocation.

"Trevor, no!" Gwen screamed from the porch, her voice like a high violin note, resonating through the mist. "Don't get hurt. It's not worth it!

"Trevor turned back and hissed at his wife. "Get back inside!"

The man was waving toward the house, with a frightening grin on his face and mouthing something, but Trevor could identify no sound. Trevor stopped two feet from the man, on whose face the grin had fallen away.  "You listen to me," Trevor muttered, fists balling at his side. "You're this close. You know what I mean? I don't care if they arrest me, I don't care if they put me away forever, if you don't leave her alone, I'm going to kill you. Understand?"

The man continued waving at the house behind Trevor as if he had not heard a word, or didn't give a damn and then crossed his arms, as if he'd done what he came for.

"Come on, be a man!" Trevor challenged. "Take a swing. Hit me if you dare."

The man slowly uncrossed his arms and Trevor braced himself. Here it comes he thought. His heart flexed and an ocean crashed in his ears. He could feel the chill adrenaline race through his body like an electric current.

The man turned and ran. It took Trevor a few seconds to realise what had happened, or more accurately not happened.

"Bastard! Come back here." He was racing across mossy clumps and hillocks and Trevor was close behind. For a while he kept pace but at forty three he didn't have the stamina or athleticism of his quarry.  The man pulled away and disappeared into the gathering moorland mist. Winded, his side cramping fiercely from the run, Trevor made his way back to the house. Gasping for oxygen he clambered into his car and shouted, "Gwen, lock the doors I'm going to find him."

She protested but he ignored her and sped away into the night. Half an hour later, having driven round aimlessly to no avail, he returned home. He found her in tears. She sat in the living room with the curtains drawn and a kitchen knife in her hand.

"What?" Trevor demanded. "What's going on?"

Gwen said, "I'm sorry, I thought it was best."

"What?" Trevor strode forward, dropping onto the couch, gripping his partner by her shoulders. "Tell me!" he cried.

"He came back," Gwen said. "He was by the bush, and I went out to talk to him."

"You did what? Are you crazy?" Trevor shouted, shaking with rage and fear at what might have happened.

"I was afraid for you. I was afraid he'd hurt you. I thought maybe I could be nice to him and ask him please just to go away."

Despite his horror, a burst of pride at her courage popped inside of him.

"What happened?" he asked.

"'Oh, it was terrible."

The feeling of pride faded and he sat back, staring at Gwen's white face. Trevor whispered, "Did he touch you?"

"No ... not yet."

"What do you mean yet?" Trevor barked.

"He said..." Her tearful face looked at his, "he said that when it's the next full moon, that's when women get a certain way because of their, you know, monthly thing. The next full moon, he's going to find me wherever I am." Her face grew red in shame. She swallowed. 'I can't say it, Trevor, I can't tell you what he said he'd do."

"My God."

"I got so scared, I ran back to the house." Gwen turned toward the window and added, "and he just stood there, staring at me, kind of singing, but I couldn't hear properly. I locked the doors right away." She nodded at the knife, setting it on the table. "I got that from the kitchen just in case. Then you came back and when he saw the car lights he ran off. It looked like he was headed across the Moor."

Trevor grabbed the phone and slammed his finger onto the speed dial.

"This is Trevor.." He was interrupted.

"Yes sir, is it the man again? The voice asked.

"Walker, now!" he demanded.

A pause. "Hold, please."

PC Walker came on the line. "What's going on, I've had several calls about disturbance up on the Moor in your area?" asked the young policeman.

"He's been here again. This has to stop now. He's said things to her, about what he's going to do."

"It's still just words, Trevor. It's the law. We'll keep an eye on your place."

"You know what you and your law can do? You can go straight to hell"

"Trevor, I've told you before, if you take things into your own hands, you're going to be in serious trouble. Now good night." PC Walker cut the line.

Trevor jammed his phone down and almost broke it again. He shouted to Gwen, "stay here. Keep the doors locked."

"Trevor, what are you going to do?"

The door slammed so hard a pane cracked and the fissure lines made a perfect spider-web. Trevor parked on the lawn, narrowly missing a Quad Bike and a four by four. Pounding on the front door, he shouted, "I want to see you. Open up!"

He hammered away for what seemed an eternity until it was obvious that nobody was going to respond, so he decided to force his way in. He stepped inside. The house was a mess. Food, dirty plastic plates, beer cans, piles of clothes, magazines and newspapers were strewn all around. There was a strong animal urine smell too. He walked down a dark corridor toward a bedroom. Something, old food, it seemed, crunched under his feet. Trevor stepped back and slammed his foot into the door. The door crashed open and Trevor stepped inside, flicking on the light. He stopped, astonished. In contrast to the rest of the house, the room was immaculate. The bed was made and the blankets were pulled taut. The desktop was ordered and polished, the rug vacuumed. Bookshelves were neat, and all the books were alphabetized. On the wall were posters showing highwaymen in a variety of poses, complete with pistols drawn and pointing. There was a model of a stagecoach and pictures of a strawberry mare, taken from various angles.

Trevor reached for the door to a walk-in wardrobe, but found it was locked. He made short work of the wooden panels and stood speechless at what was in front of him.  In the middle of the floor he saw the main attraction: an altar dedicated to Gwen. He cried out in horror as he dropped to his knees, staring at the frightening tableau. Several photographs of Gwen were pinned to the wall.

They must have been taken when she was out on the Moor riding in preparation for the Golden Horseshoe. Other pictures showed her walking, dressed in her riding gear, with the Moor as a backdrop. In one she was turning and smiling off into the distance. In another, the one that struck him like a fist, she was bending down to tie her shoe, her jeans tight enough to be a second skin. This was the photo at the centre of the shrine.

He lost control and stormed out through the front door. "Where are you?" he cried. "Where? You bastard."

The peaceful dusk over Exmoor had tipped into peaceful night. Trevor saw nothing but faint houselights dotted across the wilderness and he heard nothing but his own voice, dulled by the mist, returning to him from a dozen distant places. He leapt into his car and left long black worms of skid marks to bear witness to his anger.

Three hours later he returned home. The bright security lights were on, one of them trained directly at the offending bush.

"Where've you been?" Gwen demanded, "I've called everybody I could think of trying to find you."

"Driving around, looking for him. Is everything okay?" he asked.

"I thought I heard somebody in the work shed about an hour ago, rummaging around," she said. "And?"

"I called the police and they came by. Didn't find anything. Might've been some animal. The window was open. But the door was locked."

"Did you find him?" she asked.

"No, no trace. At least I hope I put the fear of God into him so we'll have a few days' peace." He looked around the house. "Let's make sure everything's locked up."

Trevor walked to the front door and opened it, stepping back in shock at the sight of a dark form filling the doorway. Gasping, he instinctively drew back his fist. "Whoa, hold on, take it easy," PC Tony Walker stepped into the hallway light.

Trevor closed his eyes in relief. "You scared me," he gasped.

"Actually, you scared me too," answered the young policeman. "Mind if I come in?"

"Yes, yes, please do," Trevor snapped.

Walker entered, nodding to Gwen, who ushered him into the living room. He declined coffee. He sat on the couch and said simply, "your ex husband was found dead on the Moor about half an hour ago."

Gwen gasped. PC Walker nodded grimly, but Trevor didn't even bother to keep the smile from appearing on his face. He looked up at the ceiling and mouthed a silent prayer of thanks. Walker kept his face emotionless. He looked back to his notebook.

"Where've you been for the past three hours, Trevor?" he asked. Trevor knitted his fingers together but then decided it made him look guilty and he unlinked them.

"Driving around," he answered. "Looking for him. Somebody had to. You weren't."

"And you found him," PC Walker said.

"No, I didn't find him."

"Well, somebody certainly did. Trevor. You took off chasing him."

"Well,"…..

"And then we've had reports of you chasing all over the place like a madman. Also, his house has been broken into and some damage has been done."

"I admit I broke in. You must understand, I found things there. Pictures of Gwen. He'd made an altar type thing."

Gwen's hand rose to her mouth.

"And then?"

"I drove around looking for him. I couldn't find him, so I came home. Look, I'll admit I said I would kill him but I didn't do it, because I couldn't find him. I'm not sorry he's gone though."

Gwen was frowning as the policeman continued. "It looks like he was run over by something. The strange thing is that it's only a single wheel mark. It must have been thin and heavy, because it made a channel across his head. He didn't have a chance. We need to ask you some more questions."

Trevor looked out of the window and happened to catch sight of the bush. He could have sworn there was something or somebody out there.

"I don't think I want to say anything more until I've got a solicitor with me."

"That's your right," said PC Walker, "but we need to go to the station and get this sorted out." He slipped the handcuffs on as he intoned the obligatory caution.

He was getting into the back seat of the car and as the constable was pushing his head down to make sure he didn't bang it, Trevor glanced at the bush for the final time. There, as plain as the nose on his face, stood a highwayman in full regalia with pistols drawn and his eyes glinting in the moonlight through his mask. The figure calmly mounted a strawberry mare, took one last look at Trevor, and walked his horse onto the Moor. By the time Gwen had followed the direction of Trevor's gaze, the figure had disappeared.

Gwen was left alone in the house. She opened the kitchen door and beckoned in the two men who had been standing in the shadows outside.

"That went well. I can't thank you enough. You've been incredibly brave," said Dennis.

"I'll echo that," said Vince. "We've been after him for longer than I care to remember. We'd also like to thank you for managing to keep our identities to yourself."

"Yes, that's been absolutely vital. It means we can continue our work. We can rely on your continued discretion, I hope?" asked Dennis.

"Of course," Gwen gave the men a gracious smile.

"One thing I'd like to know, though," said Dennis. "Who was the figure by the bush?"

Gwen treated them to her best enigmatic facial expression. "I don't really know," she replied, "but there is a strange legend around here about a highwayman named Faggus who rode a strawberry mare. Apparently, he escaped execution sometime in the sixteen hundreds and now roams the Moor on his horse. They also say he escaped from the stagecoach which was taking him to be executed and that is sometimes seen as well. It's probably all nonsense, but you can never be absolutely sure, can you?"

Dennis and Vince said their goodbyes. Gwen watched them drive away through the window and waved. They could not know that she was waving at the bush rather than their disappearing car lights.

PC Walker drove to the agreed rendezvous and turned out his lights. He left the engine running for warmth, but pushed a button to lock the doors.

"What's going on?" asked his prisoner, immediately worried.

"I'm waiting for someone. Well, two people actually."

"Who?" The voice from the back seat was tremulous and fearful.

"Nobody I know personally, but I've heard about them," answered PC Walker. "I've been told they know you, though."

Before long a car's headlights appeared in Walker's rear-view mirror and gradually became larger and more intense. Walker waited for the signal. The newly arrived car parked behind his and flashed its headlights once. PC Walker then pushed the button to unlock the doors, but made no other move. The offside rear door was opened and the prisoner dragged out. He looked at the face of the man responsible and his knees buckled. PC Walker had been correct, he knew them and it scared him to death.

"Thank you, constable. Most helpful. Your Sergeant will be told of your valuable assistance. There's no doubt your career has taken an upward turn tonight. Please say nothing to anybody, not even colleagues, about what's happened this evening or your career will go in the opposite direction."

"Don't worry, it's been a pleasure. I hope he helps the overall picture." PC Walker didn't risk a glance backwards.

"Oh, have no fear. It's a long journey and by the time we get him back to our place, we'll know all we need to know. You'd better get to the prize giving at the White Horse; I believe they need you there. Thanks again."

The rear door was slammed shut and the two figures, one in handcuffs and barely able to stand through complete and mortal fear, withdrew to the car behind. PC Walker drove away and pointed his car to a happier place.  He was glad to be rid of the prisoner, but much more pleased to be moving away from the other two men.

## PRIZE-GIVING

### -24-

"Ladies and gentlemen, let us begin. Firstly let me thank you for being here this evening. I hope it proves a fitting conclusion to a wonderful competition. Apart from the central business of prize-giving, there are one or two other matters that I need to tell you about. But first, I would like you to listen to something."

The room settled to an anticipatory buzz. The violin began and took over everything. The quality of the sound, the power of the playing, and the magnificent eloquence of the music completely captivated the entire gathering. The musician couldn't be seen as he was behind a curtain at the front of the room. It had been his only stipulation. He played for a full ten minutes, which is a long time as a soloist, and when he finished not a sound could be heard. There was stunned astonishment in the room.

"I'll tell you about that after we've presented the prizes," said Miriam, "but I think you'll agree it was incredible."

It took almost forty minutes to hand out the awards. Lisa and Karen were given their Gold awards in the Exmoor Challenge and their supporters banged the tables in recognition. Kevin's chest swelled with pride at his wife's achievement and he almost hugged the breath out of her when she returned to her seat beside him. Lisa and Karen winked at each other with mutual admiration and satisfaction for a job well done. Tamsyn had the honour of being the final recipient because she was the only successful competitor in the toughest category, The Golden Horseshoe. The entire gathering stood and applause filled the room as the deserving, and extremely sore, winner walked back to her seat.

"Well, I must say how pleased we are that this year has been such a success. The fiftieth running of the challenge has proved remarkable in many ways and I should explain them to you.

The sharp eyed amongst you will have noticed that there are some small horseshoes on the table in front of me, and one particularly large one. I am proud to tell you they are all gold; not gold plated, actual solid gold. Each has been engraved with the winner's name and the name of the horse as well. The winner in each category will receive a Golden Horseshoe to celebrate the fiftieth running of the event. The final prize lies in the gift of the judges and will be awarded to a person who has made a special contribution to the success of this year's event. This has all been made possible by the generosity of a particular sponsor, who wishes to remain anonymous. I think you will agree, however, that he or she deserves a round of applause as a sign of our gratitude. I would also like to thank our well known local blacksmith and farrier, Mr Oliver Benson, who has worked tirelessly to produce these wonderful horseshoes, and get them engraved in time for this evening."

Another outbreak of clapping interrupted Miriam as the popular man stood and bowed to the assembly. Miriam Huntley-Smythe then presented the prizes to the winners in each category. Tamsyn Carter, as the only finisher in the Golden Horseshoe Challenge, was thrilled to win and forgetting her sore backside for a brief moment, positively skipped to the front and then skipped back again, accompanied by much laughter and cheering.

"And now we come to other matters," Miriam said in an ominous voice. She waited for her dark words to hit home. "There are things that have been happening behind the scenes and I need to tell you about them. Firstly, many of our local farmers have been struck by theft over the past few months.  In particular, you will be aware that Quad Bikes have gone missing.  The police have, of course, been involved but recently a group of farmers got together and hired somebody to help them on a professional contract.  That man insisted on working alone. I can't go into detail about how he worked, but the results have been amazing.  All the Quad Bikes have been recovered and the two culprits apprehended.  The police helped by dashing around the Moor with their sirens screaming and blue lights flashing.  I understand that was part of the plan as it drove the culprits to ground, so to speak.  To cut a long story short, the two villains have been made to clean the Quad Bikes and to do unpaid work on the farms from which they stole every day for a year.  The farmers declined to have them prosecuted as they saw more benefit in making them work off their debt. If they fail to turn up, fail to work, or indeed do anything untoward, they will be arrested and prosecuted. Their names would then become public knowledge.  It's rather like old fashioned justice, without the physical harm.  I think it's a neat solution."

A murmur travelled around the room as people digested what they had heard.

"The community is therefore indebted to Mr Quentin Legard. Please come forward Mr Legard.

He made his way to front slowly and Miriam Huntley-Smythe shook his hand as he arrived at her side.

"We would like you to accept this gift as a token of the appreciation of this community," she said and pressed a small golden horseshoe into his other hand. He responded by whispering quietly to her. She had to lean forward to hear what he was saying.

"Ladies and Gentlemen, I have been asked to tell you that Mr Legard would like to donate his fee from the farmers to a charity called Balls to Cancer. Would Mr Kevin Wilson please come forward and receive the cheque?"

Kevin was shocked at the turn of events.  He had not told anybody about his illness since coming to Exmoor for the challenge.  He looked at his wife, who rose to her feet and began to clap loudly, full of pride for her beloved and brave husband. He received the cheque, but did not look at it for fear of seeming greedy.  When he got back to the table he looked at a cheque made out to Balls To Cancer in the sum of £25,000.  There was also a note which said, 'I was touched by your story.  As you will have gathered I undertake professional contracts and the local farmers hired me to do a job. They have agreed that I may donate their fee to your charity.  I hope it helps in some way. Best wishes, Quentin.'

Standing behind Kevin and Karen, one of the farmers who had hired Legard whispered to another. "Legard's cheque is for £25,000. We paid him £15,000. He's paid the rest himself. I wonder why."

Lisa Richards was confused. Quentin Legard sat beside her with a peaceful smile on his face and her hand in his on his thigh.

"Quiet please, Ladies and Gentlemen," Miriam started again. "There has also been another significant happening during these few days. You may know that one of the local churches has been trying to raise money to install heating, so that we may all be more comfortable during services. You may also have noticed that two gentlemen from Manchester have been here this week, ostensibly looking at and preparing for the job. Despite what you may have been told or assumed, they are not electricians; they are senior policemen investigating large scale nationwide theft and fencing of gold and other valuables. We know them only as Dennis and Vince. They knew the Golden Horseshoe was too tempting a target for the criminals they were seeking to arrest. They contacted me as organiser and asked for our help. Obviously, I was only too pleased to assist and our hosts at The White Horse, Peter and Linda were also recruited."

The room was silent as people listened intently, eager for more detail, and scoured the room for the two men. They were noticeable by their absence.

"We knew that the Golden Horseshoe prizes were valuable so exchanged the bag containing the valuables for an identical one, containing similar gold painted items. I picked up the false bag when I left the White Horse and Peter picked up the real one, which he put in the hotel safe. He delivered it to our blacksmith earlier today for the engraving work, and I collected it on the way here. Nobody noticed the swap. Unfortunately, I was attacked by a mugger who believed I was carrying the real gold and that is an experience I would not wish to repeat. Luckily, our friendly local PC came to my rescue. Again, I can't divulge all the details but I am able to say that PC Tony Walker saved the day. In the course of his enquiries he also arranged for the magnificent violin player this evening. He won't tell me the details, but let's just say it's a form of community service.  It seems to be a common theme tonight. Please, Detective Constable Walker, Tony, join me at the front."

PC Walker did not welcome the attention.  He had succeeded in his ambition to become a plain clothes officer and now he was to be publically feted and no doubt his picture would appear all over the media. He had little choice, however, and reluctantly made his way to the front of the function room.

"The judges are pleased to announce that the winner of the special Golden Horseshoe is DC Tony Walker. Without his prompt, somewhat unusual and inventive actions, we may have been here this evening staring at a bare table."

He was handed the solid gold award and, amid the blinding flashes of cameras and phones, the room exploded into thunderous applause. He couldn't wait to return to his seat at the back of the room but it wasn't anonymous any more.

"Oh, I almost forgot," Miriam Huntley-Smythe said, holding her hands in the air in an appeal for order, "The reward money which had been offered for the return of the genuine gold prizes will be donated to the church to cover the cost of the heating. The work will begin tomorrow."

Miriam Huntley-Smythe finished her peroration and sat emphatically down. The room burst into spontaneous applause and excited chatter. The Golden Horseshoe's 50th running had been a huge success and the community was stronger than ever. She had, however, deliberately omitted to announce that one horse and rider had gone missing and were still unaccounted for. The rider's name on the entry sheet was MR T F Fag and his horse was Gus ESM, otherwise known as Tom Faggus and his horse, the Extraordinary Strawberry Mare. Exmoor had added to its already rich pantheon of mystery and legend.

The room gradually emptied as excited people made their way out. Some went to the restaurant to relive their triumphs and disappointments whilst others headed for the bar. In the restaurant the American party were recounting their fishing trip. The size of their catches increased as the evening wore on and the alcohol took effect. They also hit upon the idea of having a competition to find out who could tell the most amusing anecdote or joke. The problem was that they had become quite loud and the whole of the restaurant was treated to their comedy. Jake, who, at their specific request, was again their designated waiter for the evening, came and went dutifully and smiled inwardly at what he was hearing. He asked them to try to rein it in a little, but they didn't pay him any attention, so he just stood discreetly to one side and listened.

At a table for two, discreetly placed in a corner by a window, Ray Quinn's wife Nancy put down her cutlery and said to her husband, "I think I'll enter the Golden Horseshoe next year. I'll need your help, though."

It did not sound like she was making a request. "Oh no. You enter if you want to, but I've told you before, I am not going anywhere near horses. I have my motorbike. I can control that." He had never been used to losing control of anything and now, he thought to himself grimly, he was about to have two elements beyond his control: his wife and her bloody horse. He munched on his melt in the mouth steak and let silence hang between them.

"Well if you're determined to spend time doing that I'll have to amuse myself somehow," he said. "Do you remember a certain policeman by the name of Detective Chief Inspector Sandy Lane? I might have mentioned him some time ago. He was involved in that nasty business with John Lomax and Leanne. I recall he came here to the Exmoor White Horse a long time ago.  He hadn't risen to the giddy heights of his final rank, of course, but I have always suspected that he left something here. He told Lomax about the place and how he'd hidden a package in the room he stayed in. Perhaps I'll dig around and see what I can find out. Peter, the owner seems a good man, so I'll have a quiet word with him first. Perhaps he'll be able to help set me on my way."

Quinn's wife looked at him, continued eating and chose to say nothing. She hoped he was only teasing her. She knew there was nothing she could do to stop him once he had made up his mind. She had prayed that he would retire properly once they became established, but deep down she knew that had only ever been a foolish and forlorn hope. He is what he is, she thought, and he won't change. But she loved him nonetheless.

A few people made their way out into the cool May evening air, climbed into their cars, and carefully drove away.

From wherever they were, in the bar, the restaurant or outside, nobody noticed a stagecoach on the road on the other side of the river from the inn, with its door open. A few yards away a strawberry mare turned its head as its rider, dressed in highwayman's attire and wearing an enigmatic smile, nudged it forward into the night.